SAVANNAH RUN

THE METROPOLITAN COLLECTION BOOK 1

MICHELLE DONN

MICHELLE DONN

CONTENTS

Savannah Run

First Edition

Copyright © 2020 Michelle Donn

Editing by Mistress Editing

Proofreading by Pixie Styx Editing

Cover design by Mayhem Cover Creations

PROLOGUE
DECEMBER

MR. LUCIO COPPA was a naughty boy, Leia thought as she worked on balancing his business ledger. He had money moving all over the place. At least her new job at Marino & Associates wasn't going to be as boring as she thought.

The only reason for this level of complexity in a private business was to hide funds from your soon to be ex. She was intrigued. Untangling this kind of bookkeeping mystery had been her specialty at her previous forensic accounting firm. Time to do a little snooping.

She pored over the digital client file and spotted more red flags: a foreign shell company and several large wire transfers to numbered accounts. In a divorce, his wife's attorneys would murder him in court if they found his double-dealing.

She pulled up Google to see what she could learn about Mr. Coppa. If he really was about to get a high-profile divorce, her boss might be pleased that she took the initiative to clean up this financial mess.

Impressing her new boss would be great. She wanted

him to respect her abilities. When she was laid off from her previous job at Gladwell & Smith, her rent and other bills had piled up. Living in New York City was expensive.

When she looked at the search results, Leia thought there must be two Lucio Coppas. No way Lou, owner of a profitable chain of dry cleaners, was in the mob. Yet the Metro section of the Post website had dozens of stories about his ties to organized crime. Reexamining the file's blatant accounting irregularities, she realized it could be money laundering.

Someone at Marino & Associates had to have created this elaborate system for Coppa.

Leia picked the file up from her desk and cautiously approached Marvin, her company mentor. She didn't want to jump to any conclusions.

"Marvin, you have a minute?"

"Sure, what's up?" Marvin asked, his ever-present grin lighting up his face. He indicated she should take a seat in a nearby chair.

"I have a ledger from the Coppa file, and I noticed a few irregularities. Can you take a look?"

Leia pulled up the chair and sat next to Marvin behind his desk. She laid out her worries, skipping over Mr. Coppa's mob connections. Marvin, leaning back in his chair with arms crossed, was quiet as she explained everything. His expression slowly turned more serious.

"Leia, I have been here a long time. It's a great company. Good pay, easy commute, nice people. But you can't worry about the complex transactions. That's Sal's area of expertise." He rested a hand on her arm. His tone sounded like that of a concerned father as he laid out the expectations for a new Marino & Associates employee. "You just balance the ledger and keep your head down."

Leia understood what was left unsaid: if she wanted to

keep her job, she needed to turn a blind eye to what she'd found.

Numb, she stood, thanking Marvin for his time, and returned to her desk across the aisle.

Leia looked at the other client files on her desk, the unease growing worse. The tab on the top file had the name of a notorious construction company owner whose family had generations of well-known mafia connections. It felt like she was in a movie, it was surreal.

Below that, the third folder belonged to a charming Latino man she'd just met the other day. He'd flirted shamelessly with all the ladies on staff when he was in the office. She remembered his sexy smile and smoldering eyes. She cautiously typed his name into the search bar on her web browser. The internet results included articles on his ties to a Colombian drug cartel.

What was going on at this little Brooklyn accounting firm?

Leia's ears filled with white noise as she tried to process everything. Images of her first few weeks of employment flashed through her mind—Sal, her friendly boss who took long meetings in a closed office with a Colombian drug lord. Client files with encrypted folders on the company server, and the biggest paper shredder she'd ever seen.

She should quit. Walk right into Sal's office and just be done with this company. This wasn't her problem; there were other accounting jobs.

She looked around the office. Twenty or so employees with their heads down working hard. If this wasn't her problem, was it their problem? Their ethical responsibility? Or hers.

Her heart fluttered; she couldn't walk away. She wouldn't be a bystander who let crimes go unreported. Her family had lived with the consequences of cowards who did their jobs without courage; her mother paid the ultimate price. She had to step up. The risk would be worth the reward—justice.

She could be the one that made a difference to a person, a family, society.

Leia logged into her online cloud storage account and copied over Lucio Coppa's ledger file from the company server. Her pulse throbbed in her ears. She'd just saved the first piece of evidence against her boss.

ONE

MARCH

"HELLO, my dear. I'm here for a meeting with your boss, but I couldn't pass up the chance to make a beautiful young woman's acquaintance." His voice was deep, and his Slavic accent heavy.

Leia looked up from the spreadsheet on her computer, pushing her long hair behind her ear. The man in front of her desk was big; she had to tip her chin up to meet his gaze. Middle-aged with a greasy bald head, he had a few faded Cyrillic tattoos sneaking up his neck above the open collar of his black shirt. A heavy gold ring flashed on his pinky finger, and an equally gaudy gold watch adorned his thick wrist.

Leia cleared her throat before answering. The man's presence made her feel like she was walking alone in a dark alley.

"Hello, sir?" she replied, her voice pitched just a bit higher than usual.

He hovered over her desk, leaning close, resting his hands on the Formica top. His pale eyes lingered on her modest cleavage, making her skin crawl. "I like that you call me sir, *kotyonok*."

His musky cologne was thick and swirled around her, making her nose wrinkle in distaste.

"May I help you with something, sir?" Her cheap office chair squeaked as she pushed it back, putting as much distance between herself and the large man as possible. The hair on the back of her neck tingled with unease.

He stepped around the side of her desk, his gaze sweeping over her lean legs and stopping on her sensible shoes.

"These magnificent legs should not be stuck behind a desk. I could make you a better offer than working here." A predatory smile curved his fleshy lips.

Reaching out, he dragged the back of his hand down Leia's arm. The rough skin on his scarred knuckles snagged on the delicate fabric of her conservative blouse. Leia's gaze followed the path of his hand down her arm. She suppressed the urge to shudder.

She'd always thought snap judgments about someone's character were useless, yet she was sure her visceral fear of this man was warranted. She couldn't stand his touch; she jerked her hand away and placed it on her mouse.

He chuckled. Leia stared at her computer screen, avoiding his eyes.

"Ah, Pavel, I see you've met one of our most brilliant accountants, Leia Stone. She's a CPA from U Penn." Sal Marino, Leia's boss, walked up to her desk. Next to the big Russian, Sal seemed almost delicate.

Gesturing at the man, Sal told her, "This is our newest client—Pavel Oblonsky. Big import/export businessman. We're thrilled to have him as part of the Marino & Associates family."

Sal clapped Oblonsky on the shoulder and propelled

the big man toward his private office on the other side of the open office space.

Oh, God, no. Sal has another dirty client.

"Hey Leia, are you okay? You're white as a sheet," asked Marvin from the desk across the aisle. He looked concerned, glancing at Sal's office door. He could tell that Oblonsky had unsettled her.

Marvin always reminded Leia of a kindly uncle that helped you sneak an extra helping of dessert when Mom wasn't looking. Even though he overlooked the wrongdoing at the firm, he was a good man.

"Ah, I'm okay. That client—" She stuttered to a stop, not sure what to say to Marvin. Her mind was swirling; she rubbed her hands up and down her arms like she was warding off a chill.

"Hey, I get it, my daughter is your age, and that guy was in your space. Want me to ask Sal not to assign you to his account?"

"No, it's fine, I've got it. I don't want Sal thinking I can't handle a situation, but thanks, Marvin." She focused back on her computer screen. She would put up with Oblonsky's awful presence in hopes she could get into his file. She knew her gut reaction to the man was a huge red flag.

Leia straightened in her chair, ready to research the newest member of the Marino & Associates family. She clicked open a new search window on her computer and typed in his name.

The first result was from The New York Post website; the headline proclaimed: "Russian Mobster Walks, Botched Port Authority Investigation." She clicked on the glowing link; the gruesome news story filled the screen. She read the details and was sure if she had looked pale before she must look even worse now.

Yesterday Pavel Oblonsky walked out of a mid-town courtroom a free man. Prosecutors dropped all charges against him stemming from the July human trafficking tragedy at the port of New Jersey. Oblonsky, a long-suspected member of the Russian mob, was accused of multiple counts of human trafficking and manslaughter.

TWELVE WOMEN, all Russian nationals, died while imprisoned in a shipping container that was trapped in port for weeks during a Teamsters union strike. The women succumbed to dehydration, more victims of international human trafficking. Prosecutors were unable to proceed due to a lack of cooperation from Russian authorities and the mishandling of the investigation by the port authority.

LEIA CLICKED on the first photo, and an image of inside the shipping container filled her screen. Bedding and discarded clothing littered the narrow metal box. She counted five large clear plastic containers that must have held water for the women; all of them were empty. She vividly remembered how hot last July had been; a shudder passed through her.

THE NEXT PHOTO had a single woman's shoe in the foreground. The red shoe in sharp focus was on the ground next to the steel container. Behind it, a row of twelve black body bags filled the frame. The two photos burned her eyes, and the horror those women had been through made her chest ache. These victims deserved justice.

She quickly closed the search window, hoping no one else in the office had seen the images. She took a steadying breath and exhaled slowly, wishing she could erase the pictures from her mind as simply as she shut down the internet browser. She was feeling physically ill after seeing the photos.

For almost four months, she had been able to pretend she wasn't part of helping them break the law while she slowly collected information for the FBI. But Oblonsky's vile presence and evil deeds couldn't be ignored. She had promised herself that by the end of tax season, April 15th, she would have enough information to ensure that the FBI would not only listen to her but protect her. Her timetable needed to accelerate.

She wouldn't walk away from her commitment. The sleepless nights, the stress every time she added a file to her stash of evidence, it would all be worth it when she presented her information to the FBI. At the office, she felt isolated from her co-workers. Loneliness and bouts of uncertainty plagued her, but she needed to finish what she'd started. She owed it to her mother's memory.

She opened her cloud server application on her phone, clicking the folder where she saved her evidence, and only sixteen files were listed. Only sixteen files. She ran a hand through her long hair, clutching the roots in frustration. She needed more data, and the only way to get it quickly was with unrestricted access to the company's central computer server.

She couldn't stomach working here knowing she was helping a killer like Oblonsky. She'd been pretending that these men weren't that terrible, but Oblonsky had ripped the veil from her eyes. Even if she had to do something rash, it was time to bring Sal Marino and all his dirty clients to justice.

TWO

LEIA SLIPPED into Sal's office and perched carefully on the edge of his office chair behind the big mahogany desk. The computer screen in front of her was open to the main page of the company's accounting program. *I can't believe I'm doing this.* She let out a long exhale and steadied her hands. The outer office was quiet; everyone was at the mandatory Wednesday family-style lunch in the conference room next door.

Sal's office was one of the few private spaces at Marino & Associates. It faced the back alley, and Sal always kept the blinds closed. The office was his cave; Leia had been in here a handful of times, including for her job interview. The office had dark wood paneling on the walls and decades' worth of Yankee baseball memorabilia crowed every available space. It felt like a blend of a gentlemen's club and a teenage boy's bedroom.

"I'm so not cut out for corporate espionage," she whispered, her heart racing. She arranged her long legs under Sal's low desk, ready to get to work.

Reaching into the pocket of her tailored black pants

with sweaty palms, she pulled out a brand-new high capacity USB thumb drive. After a few fumbling attempts, she had it plugged into the front of Sal's computer. The stress sweat was starting to tickle her underarms.

This idea seemed foolproof last night after a bottle of pinot noir: go in, copy the files, and leave.

She dried her palms on her slacks and reached for Sal's mouse. She opened the file organization program, navigating through the system to find a massive set of folders with client data. Her heart raced. That had to be the data she needed. Clicking in the search window, she typed in Lucio Coppa's client number. Yes! There he was.

She moved up to the parent folder and began scrolling through the items. It included all the files for Marino & Associates "special" clients like Oblonsky and Coppa. This folder was it; she found it. A tremor ran up her spine.

Oh my god. There were so many files, so many clients— more than she had ever known. A few of the names that scrolled by as she turned the knob on the mouse were high profile enough criminals that she didn't need to put their names into a Google search to know they were bad news.

With her limited file access, Leia had believed there was a small handful of *special* clients. But hundreds of files were scrolling across the screen, names of people and companies; this was far bigger and more dangerous than she dreamed.

The dread that she'd been trying to tamp down rose unbidden to the surface. These weren't the kind of men who would accept an investigation into their financial lives without seeking retribution. They would want revenge on whoever brought their unscrupulous dealings into the light of day. Leia knew copying this data would change her life —and not for the better. She stiffened her resolve.

With a trembling hand, Leia navigated the mouse,

setting the files to copy to her USB stick. She glanced at the time and realized this was already taking way too long. In about five minutes, someone, probably Marvin, would notice she was missing lunch.

The file-copy progress bar appeared, and just like that, her plan was going to fail. The bar showed an estimated 35 minutes to complete. She let out a shaky breath; this was bad.

The only way she could wait for it to finish would be to leave the computer unattended and come back. She flopped back into Sal's plush leather chair and stared at the computer screen. Her plan to copy what she needed and then go next door in time to make her plate and join the feast already in progress was a bust.

"Come on, baby. You gotta go faster." She glared at the meter.

Its progression was glacial.

Her leg was bouncing with nervous energy, and the leather desk chair squeaked; the noise frayed her nerves. She needed a better plan right now. Sitting here in Sal's office was an insane risk. Planning to come back and retrieve the fully loaded USB would be stupid. A million things could interfere.

If she abandoned the USB and Sal found it, he would destroy every shred of paper and every byte of digital evidence. He would start looking for a spy in his office. She would have no data to show the FBI, no reason for the Feds to protect her from Sal's clients. The plan would be dead in the water, and she would be out of options—her dream of bringing Sal to justice crushed.

She blinked away tears of frustration. She was so close; she was sitting right here with all the client files. Getting up from this desk and walking away with nothing was out of the question.

A bright blue icon on Sal's computer desktop caught her eye. It was the same file-sharing application that she used at home. Thinking quickly, she clicked into the program and shared the incriminating files with her username: TheAccountant93.

It was a ton of data, and copying it to the cloud would take even longer than to the USB, but she didn't need to get back into Sal's office for this to work. When she had everything, she could just delete her account on the file-sharing app to cover her tracks. The upload would be very slow, but at least it was a backup plan.

Leia closed all the windows on the computer screen but the company's accounting program main page. She took a final look at the USB drive jutting out of the front of Sal's desktop. Could she trust her backup plan to be her only plan?

She stood up and repositioned the chair just like it had been when she came into his office. After a steadying breath, she smoothed her hands over her slacks and across her clammy forehead. It was time to go. She bent over and snatched the USB out of the computer, then put it in her pocket. *This upload better work. I'm never doing this again.* She stepped out of Sal's open office door.

Slipping into the crowded conference room, she pulled out her smartphone, clicked a few buttons, and began the file upload to her secure Amazon cloud storage account. The notice on the screen said one hour until upload complete. Fingers crossed.

She looked up, closing her phone, and right into the eyes of Sal Marino. Their eyes met; he smiled kindly at her. She nodded her head and averted her eyes, reaching for an empty plate on the buffet table. A nervous blush heated her face, and she hoped he hadn't noticed her reaction. Ugh, this was the reason she never played poker.

Sal was a small man and brilliant accountant; his sharp gaze didn't miss much. He'd grown up in Brooklyn with many of his dirty clients. Leia wasn't sure if he shared their violent tendencies. Her nerves caused her empty stomach to grumble. She was suddenly starving for some comfort food.

Walking around the buffet table with the last few lingerers, she filled her plate with piles of food and tried to put the moment with her boss out of her mind.

This Wednesday's lunch was going to be a long one. Sal was in a jovial mood, chatting with everyone, checking that the team was ready for the final push at the end of tax season. Leia listened to the conversations around her with half an ear while she mindlessly devoured a plate of carb-loaded Italian food.

Lifting her cell phone off the conference table, she clicked refresh on the connection to her cloud account again. The progress bar had steadily advanced. She estimated in another thirty minutes, she would have finally succeeded in securing the incriminating data in the cloud.

She'd done it. She wasn't relieved. Instead, a thread of fear was winding its way up her spine.

Time for more manicotti. She dove back into her food.

"I just don't know where someone your size can put all that food," Marvin said, gesturing at the plate in front of Leia.

"Good thing I brought my running clothes for after work," she replied, giving him a cheesy wink that she thought seemed like something she would typically do. Today was anything but typical.

Between bites, Leia continued obsessively clicking refresh on her cloud account status. Watching as folder by folder, the file-sharing app copied Sal Marino's secrets into her secure account. Leia cleaned her plate. Even the extra piece of garlic bread that Marvin had saved for her was gone. She was a champion stress eater, and good manicotti was perfect comfort food.

Forty-five minutes of accounting talk and office bonding chit-chat later, James, Sal's office manager, brought out a massive platter of cannoli. Dessert signaled to all the employees that Wednesday lunch was over, and it was time to get back to their desks.

Leia checked her phone. Just a few more minutes and the transfer would be complete. She needed a little more time. She wanted all the data before Sal got back to his office, just to be sure.

Everyone's getting up. This is bad. Desperate, she looked to the head of the table where Sal was talking to Mark, the office baseball fanatic. Perfect! What she needed was a baseball conversation.

"Mark, are you and your buddies still planning that Florida Spring Training trip?" Leia asked as she walked up to the men.

And just like that, it was all baseball. No more accounting—the office baseball guys were roping Sal into their pre-season speculation, Mets fans talking over Yankee fans. She'd never loved *"The Game"* as much as she did in that moment. Sal was a die-hard Yankees guy. His passionate defense of his team's roster would give her more than enough time for the upload to complete. Inwardly she congratulated herself and started to move away from the baseball fans gathered around the head of the table.

BING! Leia's phone buzzed in her hand with an alert. A similar alarm sounded from the vicinity of her boss's pocket. Fumbling for her phone, she opened the file sharing app and saw the notice. *TheAccountant93 saved 376 files. Two minutes ago.*

Thankfully, Sal was currently arguing shortstops, but

he must have felt Leia's gaze. His eyes met hers as he pulled out his phone and casually clicked it to silent. She smiled, nibbling nervously at her bottom lip, hoping that Sal wasn't reading his screen and seeing the same app notice. She let out a small sigh of relief as he carelessly dropped his phone back into his pants.

She knew that those bings were breadcrumbs laying a trail that Sal could follow right to her desk; she needed to get her data to the Feds now. When Sal finally read that notification, he would know something in his files was modified. He was going to start trying to figure out who TheAccountant93 was, and if he remembered these simultaneous alert chimes, it wouldn't take him long to decide it was her.

BACK AT HER desk Leia flopped into her chair and looked past Marvin, who was still lumbering back to his workstation. Sal, Mark, and the rest of the baseball guys were finally straggling out of lunch and back to their respective desks.

This was it. She had all the data; she should be excited. The reality was she now had damning financial information about some of New York's most dangerous men in her possession. She was on her own until she met with the FBI and secured some protection. The criminals whose financial secrets she had stolen would stop at nothing to destroy the information—and her.

It was time to run and get law enforcement help. Sal headed into his office. It might only take a few minutes for him to figure out what the alert had signified. He wasn't the kind of guy to overreact; he was methodical and would take the time to look at the details, maybe get help from

James. Her chance to make a clean getaway was drawing to a close.

She opened the file-sharing app on her phone and clicked the button to close her account. "Are you sure you want to delete your account?" the box in the center of her phone screen asked. She laughed under her breath at the question. Never in her life had she been so sure she wanted to delete anything. The 376 client files were all safely stored in the Amazon cloud. If she could have kissed CEO Jeff Bezos's bald head in gratitude, she would have. An uninstalled application notice flashed on her phone screen.

Leia looked at her desk, and other than a framed picture of her and Dad on graduation day, she didn't have anything personal to take. Her father would have been proud of what she was doing today. It would've been nice if she could have told him about this, but he passed a few years ago. With him gone and her mother's tragic death more than a decade before, Leia was alone. Once she got this information to the FBI, she would toast to her mother's memory, the inspiration that drove her to turn whistleblower.

Under her desk was a knapsack with a few changes of clothes and her running gear; she brought the bag just in case her plan went sideways and she needed to get out of town. Her diligent planning had felt like overkill this morning when she was in her apartment; now, she was thankful to have a bag of stuff ready to go. Her dad had taught her to always plan for the worst. And right now, she felt like this was the worst. It was time to go.

Across the office, Sal's door burst open, and he shoved his phone at James. Waves of stress radiated off the small Italian man. The serious look on Sal's face and James's corresponding anxiety was all she needed to see. They spoke in low voices; the panic had started. They had the alert from the file-sharing app and were figuring out that their clients' confidential data wasn't confidential anymore. Sal grabbed the phone out of James's hand and fled back into his office.

"Marvin, I'm dying over here, so much pasta. I think I'm going to do a lap around the block. If I don't move, I'll just fall asleep." Leia reached for the knapsack and pulled out the running shoes with trembling fingers, shoving her heels back in the bag. "I might get a coffee. Cover for me?"

Marvin looked up from his computer screen and rubbed his paunch. "Only if you bring me back a venti latte. That was one cannoli too many. I need a hit of caffeine."

"Sure."

She felt a little bad that Marvin wasn't going to get his afternoon pick-me-up, but it was time to run. She would miss the security of having a normal life and boring job, but she couldn't pretend she was okay with helping break the law any longer. She was taking her chance to make a difference. Once the FBI had the files, she would be safe, and someday when all of this was over, she would get a new job and a regular life.

She ducked under the desk to put on her running shoes. As she tied her laces, Sal came huffing past her, his cell phone pressed to his ear. She glanced up from her shoes to see him for what she hoped was the last time not in handcuffs. Stress sweat dotted his forehead, and his hair stood on end, mussed from him running his hands through it.

"I'm going to handle it in house." He stopped at the office door, using his forearm to wipe off the sweat on his face before pulling on his coat while the person on the other side of the phone call shouted in his ear.

"Oblonsky, you're not the only one affected. I have

resources, but if I need someone in your line of work, I will be in touch." Sal hung up the phone, yanked the door to the landing open, and thundered down the stairs.

Leia clicked save on the last computer file she had open and silently counted to twenty before shouldering her knapsack and heading for the door.

"See ya soon, Marvin," she lied, wishing she could tell him to quit his job before the Feds showed up to raid the office. He'd been a good co-worker, a solid guy, and deserved better.

THREE

THE HARD BENCH in Grand Central station was as good a place as any to have a life crisis. She had a plan; she thought it was a good one. Apparently, getting in to speak with the FBI was not as simple as she'd believed.

The New York office accepted appointments for walk-ins but not actual walk-ins. The stern woman at the front reception desk had told her she could go to local law enforcement if she had information about a crime in progress. Leia wanted to cry, but the front lobby of the FBI field office didn't seem like the right place to do that, and the receptionist hadn't looked sympathetic.

There was no way she was going to the local cops; she had to guess at least some of them were dirty for Sal to have been in business as long as he had. She'd sat in front of the FBI office in Manhattan and called every FBI branch in the northeast until she was able to make an appointment for tomorrow morning in DC.

So now she was waiting for her train at Grand Central.

She hadn't counted on leaving a trail of breadcrumbs behind when she took the data. Her impulsive choice had her reevaluating her decisions. She felt like the situation was at a tipping point. Sal would figure out she was the one responsible, and he would come after her, hard. She needed to get to DC and force the FBI to help her.

Otherwise, her life was upside down. She would need skills that were outside of her realm of experience to get her life back if she couldn't get the FBI to act.

A memory tickled at the back of her mind. A pair of piercing blue-gray eyes, a quick intellect, and a job that helped people with complicated problems. At her wits' end, she thought back to her first meeting with Eric Robb.

Robb had been a client at her previous job; he mainly used the firm's advanced forensic accounting services. But last year, his regular tax accountant had moved away, and he needed to file his personal and business taxes. The April 15th deadline was looming.

Leia's boss asked her to do the job; it was easy enough for an accountant with her skills. Robb was charismatic and good looking. They had instant chemistry over discussions of withholdings and amortization tables. His career, on the other hand, was unique. He had vaguely explained his work without going into specifics.

It was her boss's comment that stuck in her head. "Eric Robb is the man to call when you've lost control of your life and need to get it back."

She had hated that Gladwell & Smith had a policy against dating the clients, or she would have jumped at Eric's coffee invitation. It was that chemistry that had prompted her to save his cell number in her phone. At the time she'd been thinking someday she would boldly call him out of the blue and see if that offer for a cup of coffee was still on the table. Well, it appeared today was that day, but she was looking for a lot more than a cup of coffee.

"THIS IS ROBB," Eric said into the cell phone.

He seldom answered an unknown caller, but the area code was in the city, so he gave it a shot. He had a free moment. Why not talk to a telemarketer? Getting up from his oversized modern desk, he walked to the wall of windows; the view of New York's East River spread before him. He spent most of his workday with his back to the spectacular scenery, focused on a sea of computer monitors. It was good to remind himself that there was a whole city outside his home office.

"Hello, Mr. Robb. I hope you remember me; it's Leia Stone. I worked on your taxes last year."

"Yes, I recall. I missed your assistance this year." He remembered the pretty brunette accountant.

When Leia's boss at his forensic accounting firm assured Eric that she could handle filling out a personal income tax 1040 form in her sleep, he was skeptical. She looked more like the girl next door than a seasoned accountant, but when she reviewed the completed forms with him, it was evident that *the girl* knew her job. She explained that she'd been working on his forensic cases for years, and untangling a complex financial system was her specialty. Smart and pretty.

Impressed, he'd asked her out for coffee. A date she declined because he was a client. Smart, pretty, and professional. She'd blushed and seemed flattered by his attention. He'd hoped she would be doing his tax return this year— any reason to look forward to filing taxes. He'd been disappointed to learn she was no longer employed at Gladwell & Smith.

"Last year you told me you're the guy people call when their whole world is flipped upside down. And that you can put it right side up again. You're some kind of facilitator for people with problems, right?"

"Yes, I'm a fixer," he replied.

Facilitator was too kind of a word to describe what he did. Eric Robb was a fixer; short of killing people, he would fix just about any problem a client brought to him. Business partner stealing from you? No problem. He would get the money back. Assets need to disappear before a divorce—what assets? Need a scandal to be swept under the proverbial rug before it could ruin a fledgling political career? Done. He was good, quiet, and very expensive. The tools of his trade ranged from computer hacking to blackmail. He would play dirty so his clients could get what they wanted.

"My life is upside down."

Eric could hear a PA system in the background. She was in an airport or train station.

"What's happened?" he asked.

"I took information…evidence that I want to turn in to the FBI. It will send people to jail. I went to the New York FBI office, and they turned me away. I didn't have an appointment. I didn't get past the front door." Her voice was a little shaky.

He hoped that she was overreacting; she was an accountant. Tax fraud wasn't usually the FBI's jurisdiction. He liked to deal in hard facts, not suppositions. He should be able to talk her off the ledge and give her some advice. Peace of mind was all she needed. Maybe revisit his offer to take her out for a drink.

"I can't afford to pay you much," she rushed to add.

"Advice will be on the house this time; a thank-you for the stellar job you did on my taxes last year. Who? Who do you have information on?"

Leia rattled off a laundry list of names. Eric let out a

long low whistle into the phone. He wasn't an expert on the criminal element in New York, but with his job, he had more than a passing familiarity with the darker side of the city.

"What kind of information?" He needed the facts.

"Money laundering, tax evasion, financial information on their illicit enterprises."

"Are they aware you have this information?"

"I'm pretty sure they'll figure it out quickly."

Aggravated, he sighed into the phone while pacing his luxurious office. If that cast of thugs knew she had damaging information on them, she was in over her head.

"You don't go to the FBI. You get to an airport and fly anywhere; then you keep going until you have a new name, in a city no one has ever heard of, in a place no one ever wants to go. I can help you with some new IDs." He paused and waited for a reply.

"I have an appointment for tomorrow morning with the FBI at the DC headquarters; it was the only field office willing to take me. I'm not missing that appointment." She was determined.

Pacing in front of his office windows, exasperated Eric ran a hand through his hair.

"Leia, you can't take on these kinds of guys. You need to hide, and once you have a hiding spot, hunker down until they forget about you. Don't be a hero. The FBI doesn't have magical powers to protect you. By the time the Feds realize you're a valuable asset, it'll be too late for you." He didn't want to think about what those kinds of lowlifes would do to a young woman to protect their businesses.

"Let me meet you here in New York or DC. I can help you craft a strategy; we can find a way to dump the info to the Feds or the press and keep your name out of it. We can get you a head start on a new life. We could set you up in Paris; it's beautiful in the spring." He could feel the conversation slipping away from him; she was going to turn him down. He felt a little desperate. This woman was the poster child for integrity, but he didn't want to see her become a martyr.

"I understand your concern, Mr. Robb, but I have to do this. I thought you might be able to offer some support for my meeting with the FBI and toward getting my life back when this is over. That's why I called."

Eric was incredulous; she had no idea. She thought this was a TV crime drama. She would walk in, drop off her evidence, and be home in her apartment after the commercial break, living her old life. If her data was half as damning as she said, she would need protection. Either the Feds needed to protect her, or she needed to be ready to run.

She continued, "I'm the only person that'll make it right. I will do this. I am going to make the FBI listen." Her conviction was growing stronger as she warmed up to defend her naive understanding of the system.

"Leia, the system is slow and inefficient…"

She cut him off. "I'm sorry to have wasted your time, Mr. Robb. My train for DC is leaving Grand Central in a few moments; I need to board. If I find a need for your advice in the future, I will call back."

She didn't even say goodbye. Just a click and the line went dead. Eric stared at the phone in his hand. *Good riddance.*

Three minutes later, he pulled up his phone to book a ticket on the next flight to DC from JFK airport.

ERIC LEANED against the large brick planter in front of the FBI's J. Edgar Hoover building, looking up from his cell phone to scan the crowd of public servants rushing to work in the ugly headquarters building behind him. Most clutched a coffee in one hand and a briefcase in the other. He shuddered in distaste, watching the mindless law enforcement drones file past. It had once been his aspiration to be accepted into the training program for the FBI; now, he couldn't imagine working for the government.

Eric straightened to his full height when he spotted a determined Leia marching across the open plaza. He took a moment to examine her, see if his memories had been accurate. She wore a generic navy skirt suit with a white blouse. Her jacket, buttoned against the slight chill in the March morning air, was nipped in at the waist showing off her lean figure. Her thin blouse was modest, open just below her delicate collar bones. Long, athletic legs ate up the pavement bringing her closer to him. The glorious chocolate hair that he remembered was smoothed back into a tight knot at the base of her neck. Such a shame to hide its beauty.

He stepped into her path, his broad frame blocking her way. She stopped short, blinked rapidly, then fixed him with a hard stare. Her flawless skin was flushed, her full lips parted. But she said nothing.

Her wide brown eyes questioned the reason for his presence even if her lips were silent.

"I came to see if I could talk you out of this."

She stepped back from him, arms crossing. It was clear she was determined to have it her way or die trying, and that wasn't something he wanted on his already burdened conscience. He held up a hand to keep her from interjecting.

"If you insist on going to the FBI, I can give you some assistance."

"Why would you come all this way to help after just one phone call?" She narrowed her eyes her and waited for an answer.

"I have a pretty heavy debt to pay karma and thought helping you would help balance my account." There was no way he could explain the anxiety he'd felt when he hung up the phone yesterday. He couldn't even explain it to himself, but he knew aiding her was vital.

She tilted her head, looking at him, examining his face. She must have been satisfied by what she saw. "So, what are you going to recommend as my consultant, Mr. Robb?"

He raised an eyebrow at the new title he had acquired: consultant. He led her over to the planter he'd been leaning against, out of the busy walkway. "What do you have to show them?"

She pulled a USB thumb drive out of her skirt pocket.

"That's not going to work. The Feds are going to be extremely reluctant to plug a stick drive from a walk-in into a company machine. We need to get some paper." He turned and began to walk; after a few steps, he stopped and looked back. "Are you coming? There's an office store just up the block. Oh, and call me Eric."

At the office store, he had Leia print a few hundred pages of the most incriminating documents on one of Marino & Associates' clients. He asked her to choose one that would get the FBI excited about the information she had. Looking at the printouts, Eric saw it was a lot of intimate financial data, and most of it meant almost nothing until he found the client name: Pavel Oblonsky.

Eric remembered the story from a few months ago about the shipping container of dead Russian girls in New Jersey. Oblonsky was an ideal choice. Leia may look naïve, but behind her innocent face, she was an intelligent woman. After the failed trafficking prosecution, the FBI would want anything they could get on Oblonsky.

"You aren't messing around, are you? Oblonsky is like waving a red flag in front of a bull. The main issue I see is as a walk-in, they're going to be skeptical. Don't give them everything. You need leverage so you can make demands." He looked into her eyes and could see she was listening.

He reached for her hand. "Do not give them that USB drive until they agree to protect you and your family. Promise me?" Touching her delicate, finely boned hand sent a wave of awareness through him. He shook off the feeling, waiting for her agreement.

She answered quietly, looking down at their joined hands. "I promise I won't give them everything until they offer to protect me, but I don't have a family to worry about."

Of course she didn't have family. No one with a family would have ever dreamed of taking on this suicidal task. She couldn't have been the only accountant at Sal Marino's firm who'd figured out he was laundering dirty money, but all the others had something to lose. He reluctantly withdrew his hand from hers and dragged it over his face. This woman was going to age him ten years in a week.

"Next, print out a list of all the dirty clients' names. Then we're done here. It's time to see if the FBI is as smart as you think they are."

FOUR

AFTER PASSING through a metal detector and doing a brief walk-in interview, they sat in a small waiting room. The drab room inside the J. Edgar Hoover building had rows of metal chairs, a single dusty plastic plant in the corner opposite the door, and fluorescent light fixtures buzzing overhead. Leia perched in a cold hard chair, and Eric seated himself next to her, his shoulder almost touching hers.

Eric was as attractive as she recalled from their tax meetings. He was a big guy—not like a football player, but athletic—and probably just over six feet tall. He looked like a lifelong jock who kept in shape with workouts that would've made his coaches proud. He had an angular profile and a strong jawline. She guessed he was early to mid-thirties.

His black suit without a tie fit in with the FBI agents, but his looked expensive. The cloth was definitely not polyester, and his slate blue dress shirt matched his eyes. He sported enough five o'clock shadow to look sexy without crossing into unkempt. His body language was reserved like he was on alert, unlike the affable and charming persona he'd worn when she interacted with him last year.

Handsome or not, he was currently treating her like a child. It was like he was waiting with her so that after the meeting he could say I told you so. She could have used an ally, but it appeared she was stuck with a skeptical chaperone.

"Leia Stone? Please follow me. I am Agent Simms." The agent welcomed them into a small spartan office just off the waiting room. He looked at Eric. "And you are?"

"The boyfriend," Eric answered succinctly.

He placed a hand on the small of Leia's back, directing her to the chair in front of the agent's desk. She hoped her shock at Eric's unexpected answer didn't show.

Leia pulled her folder of evidence out of her bag and set it on the desk, ready to spill all the details. Once she passed the information on to the FBI, she could begin to rebuild her life. Doing the right thing, stopping guys like Oblonsky, would have made her parents proud. Eric could help her resurrect her life; that was what he did.

After brief introductions, the agent started the interview. "Ms. Stone, could you tell me a bit of background on yourself? We like to know more about individuals that walk into the FBI out of the blue."

Simms settled back into his chair, hands folded, watching her intently. He could have been a TV actor auditioning for the role of FBI agent. His hair was military short, his jaw square, and his eyes roved the room, dissecting every detail of her and Eric. She resisted the urge to smooth her skirt or pat her hair for flyaways.

She felt more like she was in the principal's office than giving sensitive information to law enforcement. Her hopes for this meeting were fading fast. This man wanted to chase down bad guys in a gunfight, not wade through thousands of pages of financial records.

"I'm a CPA with a degree from U Penn. For four years, I worked at Gladwell & Smith in the forensic audit department. Last year the firm downsized, and I was let go. In the fall, I got a new job at Marino & Associates, a small accounting firm in Brooklyn, and that is why I am here."

Simms appeared unimpressed. Leia reached for her file folder. She removed and kept the client list and put the folder on the desk facing toward Simms.

"This is the confidential Marino & Associates client file for Pavel Oblonsky, the Russian mobster." The hundreds of pages of financial documents were a blueprint of the criminal organization that Oblonsky had headed for the last few decades. It also included a paper trail detailing how Sal Marino was cleaning his newest client's cash. She leaned back in her chair, waiting for Simms to react in some way to the file or the name. The agent looked at her and then back to the stack of paper—no reaction.

"It has details on Oblonsky's financial dealings for years; my boss is helping him hide his money. There are shell companies and wire transfers into foreign banks. Everything needed to trace how he launders his cash."

The agent's poker face did not waver. Leia was exasperated; she pushed the folder toward the agent. Simms still hadn't turned a page. The man's face remained expressionless.

"Can you bring in an agent in the FBI's forensic accounting division? They'll understand." As the words left her mouth, she realized how condescending she sounded.

Eric seated next to her, put a restraining hand on her leg. She turned her head and saw that he wanted her to relax, but she wasn't about to fail. Simms had to know how valuable the information was. Glancing down at Eric's hand on her leg, she tried to focus on his reassuring presence and not her growing frustration with Simms.

Leaning forward like he wanted in on a secret, Simms asked, "Ms. Stone, why are you here?"

She was about to fail; his suspicious tone told her as much. Leia blinked back tears of frustration. She tipped her head back, looking at the drab ceiling tiles above her head.

"I just wanted to do the right thing, get justice."

"For who? Are you a victim of Oblonsky or an ex-lover seeking revenge? I'm trying to understand why a young woman like you would take it upon herself to do this." Simms waved his hands toward the open file.

"You don't believe me, do you? You don't think this is real."

She could feel a hysterical laugh trying to bubble up. All the risk, throwing away her life, and the FBI thought she was a vindictive ex. She should have listened to Eric yesterday. She placed her left hand on top of Eric's on her thigh, settling her breathing using his unruffled presence as an anchor. She was glad to have a professional to rely on that would help her navigate the mess she'd created.

Leia slid the list of clients next to the open folder hoping those names would force Simms to take her seriously. Desperation was making her bold; she leaned across the desk and stabbed the paper with her finger.

"Here are the names of the rest of Sal Marino's criminal clients. I have all their data too."

Simms made no effort to read the list. She flopped back into the hard chair and looked at Eric. His face was expressionless.

"We will review what you've given us and be in touch." Simms rose from his chair and gestured toward the door. "Thank you for coming in today."

Leia removed her hand from Eric's. They had been dismissed. Eric helped Leia from her chair and guided her toward the door. Before leaving the room, he turned and plucked a card from Agent Simms's desk.

He looked at the scrap of paper. "Supervisory Special Agent." Eric smirked as he tucked the card into his wallet. "That's a pretty impressive title for a guy stuck on a desk taking walk-ins. If you want to talk to her, here's a number. We're traveling this week."

Eric passed Simms a white card with just a phone number typed across it. He then stepped close behind Leia, shepherding her to the door of the waiting area. His warm hand on her back erased the chill that the cold metal chairs had pressed into her skin. She was glad for the support.

FIVE

ERIC FOLLOWED Leia into her hotel room; she'd been quiet since leaving the FBI building. She had allowed him to bustle her into his car for the short ride to her hotel without protest. Shoulders hunched and face blank, Leia radiated defeat. She walked into the room and flopped into an uncomfortable desk chair.

The hotel was decent; it was one of the mid-price chain types that litter busy cities. The room was small but clean, with a queen bed and, on the far wall, a bathroom with harsh lighting and an acceptable sized shower. The carpet and bedspread screamed durability, not glamor.

"Have you eaten?" he asked while leafing through a surprisingly extensive room service menu. Unfortunately, there wasn't a section labeled comfort food for crushed ideals. The compulsion to take care of someone else was new, and he wasn't sure what about Leia brought it out, but he felt compelled to embrace the responsibility.

"I should eat," she replied in a monotone.

Eric proceeded to place the most calorie-laden

tempting room service order he could imagine, including cheeseburgers with fries, fettuccine alfredo, a steak, and four desserts. He was going for comfort food. He needed to get her thinking about her next move, and in her current funk, she wasn't going to be much help. If ice cream would help a woman recover from a broken heart, as his sister told him, maybe a burger could help restore Leia's confidence.

"Thank you for not saying I told you so," she said, breaking the silence while they waited for the food. Her voice was small, and she looked beaten down.

"I was just stalling until you had some nourishment. Can't kick a girl when her blood sugar is low." He nudged her shoulder with his arm as he walked past her chair.

She huffed out a small laugh, finally looking up to meet his gaze.

"I'm more optimistic about that meeting than you," he said.

She rolled her eyes. "Why? That Simms guy accused me of making up the file and thought I had slept with Oblonsky." She shuddered a little. "Have you seen Oblonsky? The idea of shaking his hand makes me want to retch. Thinking I would willingly touch any part of him is offensive."

Eric pulled out Simms's card and passed it over to her. "I may not be an expert on the FBI, but they don't waste the time of a Supervisory Special Agent on a walk-in. I think they might have already been looking at your boss; they sent Simms because they know your data is dangerous. Dangerous to you, to all those dirty clients, and to any ongoing FBI investigation. Simms was feeling you out, seeing if you were reliable."

"He wouldn't even look at what I brought."

"Oh, he looked—after we left. He had that file finger-printed, swabbed for DNA, sprayed with luminol, and who knows what else, and then he took it to the forensic accounting team for review."

"You think?" She tilted her head, considering his opinion. Her white teeth worried her plump bottom lip. He watched her pass her tongue over the reddened skin and realized he was staring. He gave his head a quick shake, getting his game face back on; she was almost a client, not a chick at a bar.

"Yeah, I do. The shitty part, excuse my language, is that until they vet you and your information, the FBI is leaving you to your own devices." That was the part causing him to worry; his livelihood was made by fixing problems, and he didn't have a plan for Leia...yet. The thought of leaving her at the mercy of the FBI made him uncomfortable.

"How long do you think it will take for them to figure out I'm for real?" she asked.

"The file you gave them was big and complex, right?"

"Yes. The method Sal is using to clean the money isn't straightforward, and if you aren't familiar with the account, it would be harder to spot the irregularities."

"That could be the biggest problem. You just gave them data, right? Not the road map to follow?"

"It's the FBI. They should be able to see what I see." She was getting defensive. He needed to feed her before the conversation went downhill.

"Room Service!" a muffled voice called from the hallway.

Fabulous.

He pulled the door wide, and the room service cart immediately crashed into his legs, knocking him on his ass.

Barreling through the door behind it was a man he'd thought was dead for the last five years—his former business partner, Max Davenport.

Stunned, Eric hesitated for a crucial moment, shocked a man he had killed was suddenly alive.

Max leapt over the cart, ignoring Eric sprawled on the ground, and jerked a large tactical knife out of a sheath on his leg, his sights set on Leia.

"Leia, bathroom now!" Eric surged to his feet, ready to fight.

Already standing, Leia scrambled for the bathroom, slamming the door shut. The lock clicked into place just before Max reached her.

Eric lunged for a large silver cloche from the room service cart, the only weapon at hand.

Max turned toward him, the vicious knife swiping at Eric's torso. When Eric blocked the strike, Max's anger took over.

The small hotel room limited his ability to counter Max's brutal attack. He swung the cloche to defend himself from the knife. Max pressed his advantage, using the weapon to pin Eric into the corner of the room between the bedside table and wall.

"Fuck the contract," Max raved, spit flying as he hissed at Eric, his eyes wild.

Eric swung the cloche blindly, slamming it into Max's right wrist. A sickening crunch followed, and the knife bounced onto the bed. Max was enraged, injured, and fighting desperately with one hand. Eric grunted as he shoved him away and into the luggage stand near the end of the bed.

"You were dead!" Eric shouted.

"Fuck you." Max got up, reaching for a gun in the

holster at his side. He fumbled with his uninjured hand to free the weapon. Eric again swung the cloche, aiming for Max's head. When the metal lid connected with his skull, the gun slipped from his fingers. Blood ran freely from the gash above Max's eye, and he stumbled to his knees.

Eric dropped the cloche to wrap his fingers around Max's throat, the past repeating itself. Eric looked into Max's eyes as he crushed his windpipe in his bare hands. Eric's adrenaline spiked, increasing his determination. Max's eyelids fluttered, and he choked, trying to find his breath.

Unexpectedly, Max lashed out, catching Eric's left knee. Eric crumbled, falling back, releasing his hold, pain shooting up his leg.

Max bolted for the exit, vaulting the room service cart and wrenching the door open with his uninjured hand. Eric turned his head to watch a dead man run down the hotel hallway before the door slammed shut, cutting off his line of sight.

SILENCE FILLED THE HOTEL ROOM; Leia cracked open the bathroom door and peered out. The brief fight between Eric and the man dressed in black fatigues had wreaked havoc in her hotel room. They destroyed the lamp and bedside table. Crushed the luggage rack. The room service cart turned battering ram was on its side in the entry. And a lethal-looking knife with a long blade and black rubber grip lay in the center of the bed.

Picking her way through the carnage and around the foot of the bed, Leia found Eric lying on the floor in the fetal position. His hands cradled his injured left knee, and a gun lay on the floor next to him. He was ashen from pain, and sweat bathed his face. Leia crouched down beside him. The aroma of the spilled food from the room service cart turned her stomach. The bathroom door had been the only thing standing between her and the violence unleashed between the two men.

She paused to steady herself before reaching a tentative hand out for his shoulder. "Eric."

He jumped at her touch, sucking in a pain-filled breath.

"Are you okay?" she asked. She'd never experienced violence up close; her father wasn't even a football fan. Her knowledge of the bodily harm humans can do to one another was limited to what's in movies. This was very, very real. And she'd brought Eric into this situation.

He groaned, and his eyes flicked open. He met her worried gaze. He gingerly straightened his injured leg and grimaced.

"Fuck me, that hurts." He lay flat on the hotel carpet for a beat, staring up at the ceiling. "Old injury from college lacrosse. It'll need a few days and some ice to recover." He was a matter of fact, like fighting for his life was commonplace. He must lead a more dangerous life than she had assumed.

Leia stood and put her hand out to help him get up. He rose to his feet, and she noticed how much taller and broader he was than her. With him standing so close, her nose was well below his chin. His size was intimidating in the wake of the violence that just occurred. But she was happy to have him on her side.

She helped him hobble over to the desk chair that remarkably survived the devastation. Once he was seated, she walked to the entry door and flipped the deadbolt and safety bar, wanting any barrier that could stop potential danger. That done, she sat on the side of the bed, her eyes fixed on the knife.

"That was for me, wasn't it?" she asked, jutting her trembling chin at the blade. She could be dead.

"Yes. I think he was sent to kill you."

Leia's breath was coming too fast; her heart raced, and panic coursed through her body. Her hands shook with a tremor of fear.

"Leia, look at me. Nothing happened; we're fine," Eric calmly told her.

"Fine! We are not fine. You're hurt, and some guy dressed like Rambo just busted into my hotel room to, to…" A sob broke free from her chest; she couldn't finish the thought out loud. She wouldn't say he came to kill her.

Dropping her head into her hands, she asked, "Why are you even here? I don't know you. You, you…" Her voice trailed off, the realization that someone had been sent to kill her blocking out rational thoughts.

"Hey! Look at me." Eric hobbled to the bedside and placed his hand on her shoulder. "We are fine. Okay?" His firm grip on her shoulder was reassuring, grounding her in the present.

She wiped at the tears fogging her view of the ugly knife still lying on the bed. She didn't have the luxury of breaking down right now. She didn't feel okay; she was terrified. Not sure if anything she was doing was right. Not sure Eric was the right man to trust. But he was the best option. Obviously, he was willing and more than capable of protecting her. He had the skills and knowledge she needed to rely on until the FBI started to help her.

He met her gaze. "I'm not going anywhere. We're going to need a plan."

She pushed away the doubts and the fear. It was time to act. A plan was something she could focus on to help her deal with what had just happened. For the time being, this was her new reality.

"Yeah, a plan sounds good." Leia sat up straighter, willing some steel into her spine. This was part of seeking justice; this was part of stepping up when no one else would. If doing the right thing was easy, Marvin or someone else at Marino & Associates would have done it. She was thankful to have Eric's support.

"ALRIGHT." Eric looked at Leia; her breathing and color were returning to normal. His hand rested on her shoulder, and he felt the slump in her shoulders disappear. The youthful accountant had more guts than most people. She pulled herself together remarkably fast. He was impressed.

He took the safety of his clients seriously, and Leia needed him more than she knew. Sal Marino wasn't messing around. Giving the contract to Max, an ex-marine and trained soldier, made it clear that Leia was an important target.

"So what now?" she asked. He withdrew his hand from her shoulder, suddenly aware of his hand lingering on her feminine shoulder.

"We need to talk about keeping you safe." Walking around the room, Eric started to restore some order to the mess. It was time to use his skills and resources to even the playing field.

"Why are you helping me?" she asked. "And don't give me a line about karma. I can't pay what you charge. I know your services are expensive. Remember, I did your taxes."

Eric paused his straightening of the destroyed hotel room; he had to tell her more about himself and his ex-partner. That conversation would be unpleasant, and they didn't have time for it right now. Bending down, he swept up Max's gun, slipping it into his jacket pocket before Leia could see. The weapon would be nice to have when they exited the hotel; he'd left his 9mm secured in the rental car along with his bags.

"I don't need money; I have more than I can spend as it is. There's a lot we need to talk about, but not right now. Right now we need to get out of here. Your boss and his buddies sent Max after you. We don't want to stick around and see what else they have planned." With Max on her trail, he felt responsible for her safety.

"Max? You know the Rambo guy with the knife?" She was back to looking nervous.

"Please, Leia, trust me until I get us to a safe place. I'll explain as much as I can then."

He was trying to understand it himself; Max was alive. Five years of guilt for a murder he didn't commit. He shoved the thoughts down. Now wasn't the time.

Eric collected their cell phones and Leia's tablet during his quick clean up. He tossed the tech into the microwave next to the mini-bar, pushing start before Leia could protest.

"What the hell are you doing?"

Nothing like nuking someone's cell phone to get them to focus.

"We're going off the grid, no cell phone or credit cards. We're a cash-only operation now." He handed her purse over. "How much do you have?"

Leia opened her wallet. "Maybe a hundred bucks?"

"We can hit the ATM in the lobby on the way out of the hotel. Max out our debit cards. I will need to use the lobby phone; I'm going to call in a favor from an old client." Scooping the fried electronics from the microwave, he stomped on them with the heel of his shoe and then dumped the crumbs in a wastepaper bin under the desk.

Stunned, she sat on the bed with her purse in her lap, staring at Eric like he had gone crazy.

"Get your stuff, Leia. We need to go, now!"

Eric pulled her up and sent her into the bathroom to get started packing.

SIX

LEIA LOOKED up at the exquisitely renovated brick house tucked next to the Australian embassy building. Three stories of multi-million-dollar real estate on Embassy Row. Massachusetts Avenue housed over a dozen embassies and was one of the most well-guarded streets in the world. Located blocks from Dupont Circle and a stone's throw from the White House, the stately home oozed opulence. Showcased in a grandiose bow window on the front of the house was a formal dining room with a sparkling brass chandelier. She could see fresh flowers in the center of the gleaming table and silk drapes pooled on either side of the window frame. Eric must have called in a pretty impressive favor to get the keys to this place. She thought of the typical safe house in a TV crime drama—a ratty hotel room on the wrong side of town.

Eric appeared from the side yard where he'd parked the rental car in the home's rear-facing garage. "Let's head inside." He jingled a key ring on a finger, his luggage in his other hand. She could tell he was still favoring his left leg but doing his best to hide the limp. She should insist he ice the injury once they got settled into the beautiful home.

Leia picked up her bag and started for the gracious main entry stairs, but before her foot touched the first pristine step, Eric's hand landed on her shoulder and directed her toward the secondary staircase leading below street level.

"We're staying in the basement?" Her dreams of sumptuous meals at the grand table and four-poster beds crashed to the ground.

At the base of the stairs, he stepped around her to fit the key in the lock.

"In DC, they call it a garden apartment. It sounds less depressing." He informed her over his shoulder with a grin as he pushed open the door. "My contact is renovating the apartment down here next month, but we can stay for a few days before her demo crew needs to get started."

He flipped a light switch on and illuminated the open living area; it was right out of the early nineties. On one side was a small kitchen with beige cabinets and peeling Formica countertops, on the other a threadbare couch and scarred coffee table. The back wall of the room housed a solid looking dining table with four mismatched chairs. On the table was a tray of wrapped sandwiches, a case of bottled water, one burner cell in a plastic clamshell package, and two brand new still-in-the-box laptops. Leia eyed the sandwiches, her stomach reminding her she was starving.

"Thankfully, Katherine was able to stop in with a few things before we came. She said there are even clean towels and sheets." Eric dropped his bag on the couch and nodded down the small dark hallway. "You can take the bedroom."

Leia ventured down the hall, finding a tiny bedroom

with the linens from the mysterious Katherine folded and placed on the foot of the bed. Flipping on the light revealed more worn nineties decor, faded carpet, and an empty doorless closet with a few bent wire hangers. Definitely not the four-poster bed she'd imagined.

On the drive over, Leia had tried to keep her focus on the landmarks crawling past the car window while Eric navigated DC traffic. She caught glimpses of the Capitol Dome and Washington Monument from the passenger window while the events of the morning replayed in her mind. A hired killer was gunning for her. If Eric hadn't inserted himself into her life, she might be dead.

Eric had done what was needed to protect her, and she was grateful. The man was confusing. Even though he was against her talking with the FBI, he'd appeared for her meeting. He was helping her run from Sal's hired hitman. And, tonight, they would be spending the night together in a safe house he had organized. She only felt safe staying in DC because he was here handling things. Alone, she would have run. She wasn't sure how or where, but that would've been her only option.

It appeared he was sticking with her. His assistance had been invaluable, but she wondered if she could rely on him moving forward. She could offer to pay him, but the kind of money she could offer might just offend him.

While in the bedroom, she changed out of the business suit she'd worn for the futile FBI meeting and slipped into a pair of yoga pants and a loose, comfortable top. She let her hair down from the tailored knot she had worn all morning, fluffing out her long brunette waves. She rolled her neck and shoulders, everything tight from stress.

The plate of sandwiches was calling her name; she headed back to the living room. Eric needed to answer some questions about his life, job, and a psycho killer named Max.

"WHO'S MAX?"

Sitting at the dining room table, a half-eaten sandwich by his elbow and a bag of ice already on his injured knee, Eric looked up at her question and stared at her like a deer caught in someone's high beams. She watched as he finished chewing his mouthful and swallowed. Leia took a seat in the chair across from him, unwrapping her sandwich, taking a bite, and waiting for his reply.

"My job is unorthodox. I fix problems for wealthy and influential people. When I first started, Max was my partner. He did most of the fieldwork. I spent most of my time at a desk or on the phone." Sliding his half-eaten sandwich away, Eric gazed unfocused at the blank wall behind her as he spoke. "Until today, I thought he was dead. Five years ago, Max went out on a job, got us in over our heads on a project. He never came back. He was dead."

Eric pulled himself together, wiping a hand down his face. Leia could tell there was a lot he wasn't telling her.

"How does one end up with your career?" Leia figured there wasn't exactly a website with job postings for something like this.

"I have a diverse set of qualifications, including a master's in computer science from MIT and a web of noteworthy contacts, and I can handle myself in a messy situation. When I finished my degree, I applied to the FBI. They turned me down because of the knee injury." He gestured to the ice pack on his leg. "I found Max online. He had skills that complemented mine, and we began to offer services to those who could afford us. I've been working alone for the last five years."

"I know you fix problems, but how?"

"I do what needs to be done." He paused, wetting his lips before he continued. "I am not a good guy. I'm more of a pragmatist. I don't set out to break the rules, but I'm more than willing to bend them as needed. I focus on the facts and then manipulate them for my client's benefit."

"Are your clients like Sal's? Drugs, women, guns?" Her bite of the sandwich turned to dust in her mouth while she waited for his answer.

"No, more politicians, businessmen, and celebrities. People that need their dirty work outsourced."

"Are you a criminal?"

He looked at her, and she could see him working out the best answer.

She choked down her bite of food. "Don't do that, Eric. Don't craft a perfect answer. Just tell me, are you a criminal? How hard can that be?"

"Well, I'm not a murderer," he said, followed by a cynical chuckle. "In your eyes, I'm not sure if I'm a criminal. I have violated plenty of laws. I threaten people with social and financial ruin on a regular basis. I lie to get what I need and occasionally steal."

He leaned forward, his eyes meeting hers, and his fingers circled her forearm that rested on top of the table. His voice was honest and a little rough from disguised emotions. "You tell me, Leia, am I a criminal?"

"I'm not sure." She returned his gaze and searched his face. His expression was sincere; the fingers he'd wrapped around her arm were gentle. She felt a connection with him and wanted to believe he was her white knight because she'd had about all she could handle on her own. He withdrew his hand from her arm; she felt adrift.

Eric sat straight in his chair, a business-like shell covering the honesty that had been in his eyes moments before. "Max implied there was a contract on your life. It's my fault he's alive to hunt you down. Until either the FBI takes you into protective custody or you let me help you disappear, you're stuck with me."

Eric reminding her that Sal had put a contract on her life was sobering. The way she saw things, if she ran now, that would be how she had to live the rest of her life—looking over her shoulder, waiting for someone to hunt her down. There was nothing Eric could do to convince her to give up this task and disappear. Bringing these men to justice and getting her life back were the same thing. The FBI was the key.

"Would you still be here if someone else had busted into my hotel room? Not your ex-partner."

"I don't do hypotheticals," he stated flatly. Reaching down next to his chair, he pulled out one of the new laptops and slid it next to her sandwich. It was apparent he no longer wanted to talk about the past.

"You said no tech. What's this?" She held up the laptop.

"Unless you've reconsidered a trip out of the country with a new identity, you need to organize that data so the FBI can see what you see. You need to give them a roadmap. I'm going to tap into the Wi-Fi next door. If anyone tracks our IP address, I think the Australian Embassy can handle whoever comes calling."

He smiled, ripping the cellophane off his new computer. "Boot that thing up, and then give me about twenty minutes and you'll be able to get to work."

"Seriously, you're going to hack into the embassy?"

A smug laugh echoed around the basement apartment, and Eric bent over the computer in front of him, his fingers flying across the keys. His lips curled in a sexy smirk.

"ENOUGH! Click save. Put down the spreadsheet and step away from your report," Eric called as he carried in the delicious smelling bags of freshly delivered Indian food and four wine bottles. He was starving.

Setting the bags down, he closed the lid on Leia's laptop with a flick of his wrist. To make room for their feast, he moved both computers to the coffee table. While he worked to open the containers of deliciousness on the dining room table, Leia searched cabinets in the kitchen. She found both a corkscrew and some mismatched wine glasses.

The afternoon had passed in companionable silence and a few pleasant and meaningless conversations. Leia had worked to make sense of the data she'd lifted from Marino & Associates while he tied up a few loose ends with a current client. Senator Ridgwell was thrilled his daughter's recent stint in rehab wouldn't become fodder for the gossip rags because Eric had *convinced* a reporter to shelve the story. Blackmailing a sleazy journalist did make the day go faster. His second project for the day was looking for any digital footprints Max Davenport might have made in the last five years. Unlike the work for Senator Ridgwell, it was fruitless.

Max had erased his past life. His new identity was perfect; Eric couldn't find a single digital crumb. Killing Max Davenport had irrevocably altered the trajectory of Eric's professional and personal life. He thought of himself as two people: the man before he was a murderer and the man after the crime. He'd been a good man that did questionable things, but after the murder, he became a bad person. Eric wasn't sure what he was anymore, but something about helping Leia made him want to find out. Her questioning if he was a criminal today had him asking himself the same thing.

Leia returned to her chair at the table. "I think this sagging cushion has reshaped my butt in its image," she complained while sliding the corkscrew and glasses toward Eric. She rolled her stiff neck a few times while waiting for him to pop the first cork and pour. She reached for the drink with hungry fingers the moment he filled it, then took a sip and sighed in happiness.

"The way to a woman's heart is a corkscrew?" Eric asked as he poured himself a glass.

"What a wise man you are. If the question is wine, the answer is always yes."

She scooped a generous helping of chicken tikka masala and rice on her plate. She popped a morsel into her mouth with her fingers and hummed in appreciation at the flavors. Even though her life was in shambles, she was pausing to find joy in a twelve-dollar bottle of wine and some take-out. He hid his smile by taking a sip of his pinot grigio, bet she'd love dinner at his favorite five-star.

He was glad that Katherine was able to settle them into such a secure location. Short of the White House, there were few places he could imagine taking Leia right now where he would be able to relax like this.

"Wine, food, carbs, I deserve all of it. I had pretty much the worst day of my life today unless you counted yesterday. So I'm going to savor every bite, probably have too much wine, and hope tomorrow is better." She raised her glass to toast to the promise of a better day. Eric followed suit, and the cheap, overfilled wine glasses met with a flat clunk.

"Cheers!" he offered in reply before digging into a carton of rogan josh.

ERIC UNCORKED a third bottle of wine and carried it over to the couch. Leia was curled up on one end, cradling her almost empty wine glass in her hand. He topped off her glass before sitting.

"I know you think I'm crazy. You think I'm risking my life for no good reason," she said.

The food and wine had mellowed her voice; she was just making an observation, not an accusation. She was right; he couldn't see the upside in risking everything to help law enforcement.

"You gave up a lot to do this for no reward."

"This isn't about a reward. It's my chance to do the right thing, make the world better." She stared into her glass. "What did I give up? A tedious job. I still have my overpriced city apartment, as long as I pay rent. I'm not a social butterfly, and I don't have hordes of friends or even a boyfriend to miss me."

"You also have a contract killer chasing after you," Eric added bluntly.

"When I first started collecting information on Sal's clients, it was a way to make me feel less guilty. I knew that the firm was doing shady things. Putting some files in the cloud helped me sleep at night. Ending up on the run wasn't my plan." Her head rolled back, and she stared up at the popcorn ceiling, her wine glass tucked between her thighs.

"What was the plan?"

She met his gaze. "I don't know, but not this. Not until I met Pavel Oblonsky. I had convinced myself to live with the drug money and the mobsters. I slowly squirreled away info bit by bit and told myself I would start digging after Tax Day, April fifteenth. I was dragging my feet. Worried about being jobless again." Looking down at her wine glass, she lifted it and took a sip; Eric could tell she was contemplating how to proceed before she spoke again.

"Oblonsky, he sells women like they're things with no free will or feelings. He came into the office, and he looked at me like I was nothing. To him, I was meat, chattel, a commodity. Even with my education and job I was still nothing to him. Keeping my boss's secret, I was just as guilty as Oblonsky. I was just as guilty as the employees that could have saved my mother's life by coming forward. If I could blame them for her death, then the family of the women Oblonsky trafficks can blame me. I had to steal the files; I had to stop being a good employee and start being a good person."

Rubbing a hand over his tired eyes, he looked at Leia on the couch; she was brave and honest. Two qualities that people aspire to, but she embodied them. He'd fixed problems for lowlife politicians, wealthy businessmen, and social climbing ingrates. It was time he championed a cause with integrity; maybe he could be a good man again.

"What happened to your mother?" he asked.

"Short version: no one was willing to lose their job, and so she died." Cynicism dripped from every word.

Wrapping one arm over Leia's shoulders, Eric pulled her against his side as they both rested back on the couch cushions. He waited for her to relax into his body then asked, "What's the long version?"

"Remember around 2017, that car airbag lawsuit? The defective airbags that were put in cars starting back in the late 1990s."

He nodded. The wheels of justice were slow.

"Mom had a new white Honda. It was grocery day. I was just a kid, old enough to be out of my car seat but still strapped into one of those booster chair things in the back."

Eric's blood chilled when Leia's voice wavered, but she kept talking.

"They never decided who missed the stop sign, Mom or the other person. It shouldn't have mattered. It was an accident in a parking lot, a fender bender. I remember the airbag, the dust in the air, and the smell of smoke from it inflating. I was scared there was a fire. The guy who we hit was at the window to apologize, I think, but then he was yanking her out of the car. I remember him cursing at the seat belt. There was blood flowing down the front of her shirt. She had a light blue shirt on, but when I looked out my window, her blouse was blood red." Wiping a few tears from her eyes, she leaned further into his embrace, her body tense against his side.

"The paramedics came. It felt like they worked on her for hours. She was lying on the blacktop, blood pooling around her. She was still and pale. The whole time I watched from my booster seat. I don't think anyone realized I was in the car until the tow truck driver pulled me out of the back." She took a fortifying sip of her wine.

Eric couldn't fathom the trauma a young kid would suffer watching a parent bleed to death; he pulled her tighter against his chest. Her unbound hair caressed his face.

"A severed carotid artery and severe facial trauma due to a foreign object inside the airbag is what the reports all said. My father ultimately was one of the members of the class-action lawsuit. Dad got a check, a big one, but he died still mourning my mom. He wanted a trial, but the settlement was all backroom deals and attorneys with nondisclosure agreements."

She exhaled, boneless, the stress ebbing away now that the story was over. Unthinking, Eric began to rub light circles over her back with his palm while she kept talking, her slight frame leaning into him, accepting solace. It felt intimate.

"When I was about thirteen, one of the TV news magazines did an episode about the recall. They interviewed employees, hid their identities, and digitized their voices. They knew about the faulty airbags, and they helped their bosses cover up the problems.

"I couldn't be one of those faceless synthesized voices begging for forgiveness from families victimized by my boss and his clients. After I meet Oblonsky, I knew I had to do something immediately. So I walked into Sal's office and took everything." Leia twisted to face Eric and raised her glass, clinking it against his, forcing him to toast to her triumph.

He refilled both their wine glasses, then pulled Leia back against him; it felt natural to have her snuggled against his side.

"You're doing the right thing; you are ridiculously brave, and I think your parents would be proud," he said.

Eric awoke just before midnight to find Leia's back pressed to his chest. Her head was pillowed on his bicep and their legs tangled at the end of the couch. Neither had seen the end of the movie they started. The smell of her hair, floral but not too sweet, filled his nose. She was lithe with long, lean runners' legs, and her perfectly curved ass pressed into him. Holding himself still, he appreciated the way she fit in his arms.

His palm rested just below the curve of her breast, her shirt a flimsy barrier between his fingers and her warm skin. Wanting Leia could only complicate their time together, but part of him thought exploring that complication might be worth it.

She'd trusted him enough to fall asleep with him. Her body was temptation personified, reluctantly he pulled away.

Eric exhaled and carefully rearranged her so he could rise from the couch and scoop her into his arms. She mumbled, rubbing her face against his chest when he stood before relaxing again into his arms.

He tucked her into the bed at the end of the hall; she shifted, snuggling into the blankets and tucking her hand under her cheek. Looking down at her sleeping peacefully in the small bed, her hair spread in alluring waves across the pillow, he ached to join her. He turned and left the bedroom before he did something stupid. Anything that happened between them would be complicated, and that was putting it mildly.

He tidied up the kitchen to redirect his restless energy. Afterward he leaned over the countertop and curled his fingers around the edge, hanging his head. Slowly, deliberately, he thumped his forehead against one of the beige upper cabinets a few times. Maybe he could dislodge the fantasies running through his mind—Leia above him, her hair cascading over them, his hands roaming her skin.

It was going to be a long night on that lumpy couch.

SEVEN

"PLEASE TELL ME THAT'S COFFEE?" Leia grumbled.

Zombie-like, she stumbled into the living room, sporting bedhead and yesterday's yoga pants. Her single-minded focus: the coffee pot.

Eric smiled, enjoying the spectacle of sleepy—and he would guess slightly hungover—Leia. Taking a sip of his coffee to hide his grin, he watched her pour her own. She grasped the mug with both hands and chugged half of it before turning to look at him.

"How much wine did we drink last night?"

"We didn't finish the third bottle. We exercised restraint."

She joined him on the couch, looking over at his laptop screen. He had her list of Sal's clients open. Her thigh pressed against his.

"I may not have had enough coffee yet to help, but I'm going to ask what you're working on." The weight of her body leaned against him as she peered at his screen. He could smell her floral shampoo.

"Finding people, following the money, it's a big part of

my job. I'm going to help you." Tossing and turning on the lumpy couch last night was good for one thing: his brain needed a problem to work on, so he focused on Marino & Associates.

She set her coffee down, rested a hand on his thigh, and gave him a small kiss on the cheek. "Thank you."

"Don't get excited yet. I haven't found anything concrete."

Eric relished the feel of her soft lips against his skin. The warmth of her fleeting caress lingered after she pulled back. He liked helping her, not because she was naïve or in over her head, but because she'd analyzed the risks and done the right thing anyway.

"Right now, you're passing the FBI so much data, and each criminal would be a different case, a different investigation. What if it's not?"

"I might need more coffee to understand where you are going." She squared her shoulders, and he could tell she wasn't wearing a bra under her thin tee shirt. He forced his gaze back to his computer. He needed to keep his head around this woman.

"I think there could be a connection. Why would half the bad guys in New York use the same accountant? I know Sal was good at cleaning money, but my gut says it's more than that."

She yawned and stretched, arching her back. Blood rushed to his groin. She cocked her head to the side, a hand absentmindedly smoothing her tangled waves, while she considered his idea. "I hadn't thought about that, but you're right. These aren't the kind of guys that would share information about their business with each other unless there was an excellent reason."

"Exactly. Is this the full list of names?" Eric asked, gesturing to the screen. She shifted for a closer look, and her breasts pushed into his arm. He suppressed a groan and the urge to touch her.

"I have another I can send with all the company names. Let me get my laptop." Leia moved back to the dining room table and plunged into work, her half cup of coffee forgotten.

He moved the computer on his lap, adjusting his erection discreetly. He tried to relax. With the couch to himself, he might be able to control his response to Leia's body enough to supply to his brain with some blood flow. He needed to get some work done on her behalf.

This was going to be a long day.

For several hours, the only sound in the basement was the clicking of computer keys. Eric investigated the relationships between Sal's clients. And Leia continued to organize the data she stole. They each took breaks to shower, dress, and even eat.

Eric didn't work in the same room as another person. Max had been gone for five years, and even before that they'd not shared an office. He talked on the phone and met with clients, but the time he spent in front of a computer was solitary. Having someone else in the room should have felt awkward, but he was energized by sharing the space with her.

She'd changed into slim-fitting jeans, a low-cut tank, and an oversized gauzy cardigan that she kept adjusting over her shoulder when it slipped. She looked like any twenty-something New Yorker, not someone who should be running from a hired killer. The laid-back outfit was a glimpse into her private world—real Leia not Accountant Leia. The line between client and something more personal was blurring with every moment they were together.

Leia looked up from her computer. "I might have

something. A code that's associated with deposits from a single bank. It isn't an ABA or SWIFT routing code that most transactions have. I searched it online and got nothing from any of the banking identification websites."

"Let me see." Eric slid the leftovers from lunch out of the way and sat in the chair next to her. The code didn't mean anything to him, either.

He jotted it down on a sticky note for reference and asked, "Do all the accounts have deposits from this bank code?"

"Yes, and I think there might be some pattern. I'm not sure yet, but I think all these guys are doing business together, and the strange deposits are payments to each other or something." Leia's gaze stayed focused on the computer screen; she clicked through another database and tugged her sweater back over the smooth skin of her shoulder.

"I've been looking at known associates for the organizations on your list, and I'm finding more than the occasional overlap. I would agree this is a network of some type."

"I feel like that code is the key," she said.

"I have an acquaintance that might be able to help us with it. He isn't the kind of guy that'll want anything to do with the FBI, but he knows more about the underbelly of the banking world than anyone not in jail." Eric tapped the sticky note on the table. "He's not going to pass your *is he a criminal* test. Are you alright with me sending him the code?"

Leia pursed her lips considering his question. "I want to trust you, Eric." Her eyes bore into him, searching his face, looking for some reassurance. "If we give your guy this code, is it going to make anything about my situation worse?"

"Leia, I would never put you at risk, especially not to

help the FBI." As the words left his mouth, he realized that they were the absolute unvarnished truth. He was committed to helping Leia and keeping her safe. If she wanted to see Sal and his client prosecuted, then he would help.

"Let's give it a try," she said, faith gleaming from her eyes.

"HANS, how is the weather in Zermatt this time of year? Any time for skiing?" Eric walked toward the bedroom, the burner cell phone in hand, making small talk with his acquaintance.

Leia tuned out the conversation and watched Eric walk, his long legs making quick work of the short hall. The jeans and soft gray henley he wore showed off his muscled frame to perfection, and the waffle-weave texture of the shirt made her want to touch him. When he turned back around, she ducked behind the laptop screen before he caught her checking him out. Hiding in a basement with Eric was far more pleasant than she'd anticipated. He was helping with the investigation and no longer encouraging her to run. Being on the same side was outstanding.

Earlier, when the lunch he ordered arrived and she was still working, he threatened to unplug her laptop to get her to eat something. It was unexpectedly nice to have someone else think about her wellbeing. It had been too long since she had someone who cared. A pleasant warmth bloomed in her chest.

Eric walked up to the dining room table and said into the phone, "I'm putting you on speaker so I can take some notes, you alright with that?" Eric nodded his head meaningfully toward the phone, making sure Leia focused on Hans.

"It's is fine with me." Hans had a heavy European accent.

She couldn't guess what country it was from, but Leia decided Hans would look like the guy from the monopoly game, complete with the monocle and pocket watch.

"The code is not a SWIFT code. It is from the Bitcoin Exchange system, a bit like the Wild West. The codes were to help with identifying a legitimate exchange, but the system fell apart when some tech company went bankrupt. The numbers were never widely used."

"Is it a dead end?" Eric asked.

"No, just a detour. You see, the bankrupt tech company, I have access to their data. I'll look this up for you, Eric, out of kindness, but this is it. No more calling."

"Hans, you know I call because you're the best."

"I email what I find. Adieu, Eric." The phone beeped, the line dead.

Leia arched an eyebrow in question. "Did you just burn up all your currency with Hans for me?"

He chuckled. "Nah, he's been telling me to stop calling for years. Coffee?"

He gestured to the machine, and she nodded eagerly. Before they could finish their first cup from the fresh pot, the burner phone chimed with Hans's incoming email.

After a quick look, Eric passed the phone to her; the email came from an anonymous account and had no subject. The message read: *Savannah Mid City Bank – proceed with caution*.

Passing Eric back the phone, she asked, "Is Hans always so dramatic?"

"No, he's a Swiss banker. He's cautious."

Leia's fingers were already flying, googling Savannah

Mid City Bank. The website was typical for a small bank. The photos other than a few of the interior of its single location were generic stock images of happy families and business people. The website banner ad proclaimed a special introductory rate on home mortgages for first-time buyers.

She turned the computer around so Eric could see. "This is the bank that Hans is warning us about?"

"Give me some time to do a background search."

ERIC KNEW he should be more focused on his research, but Leia was distracting. Watching her cardigan slide off her shoulder to reveal more of her lovely skin before she would tug it back into place was mesmerizing. And while working, she was never still. Her hands played with her hair, her bare foot would tap, her denim-clad legs crossed and uncrossed. Every time she fidgeted, he looked up to watch, cataloging every movement. About half the time, he caught her staring back. One of them would break eye contact and focus on their computer, starting the cycle over again.

He would need to tie her to the chair—and take off that tantalizing sweater—to get any work done. Who was he kidding? If he tied her to a chair, he wasn't going to waste that opportunity by returning to surfing the dark web for information on a small bank in Georgia. The image of her hard nipples pressed into her tee-shirt that morning popped into his mind. He'd do a lot more than take off that cardigan. He envisioned her tied up and at his mercy as he sucked her hard nipples. He could almost hear her begging for more. His cock twitched at the thought of playing kinky games with sweet, innocent Leia.

Eric swallowed a moan and shifted uncomfortably in his chair

He redoubled his efforts, trying to focus on the screen in front of him instead of Leia's presence. Giving up on third-party information, he went after Savannah Mid City Bank's private network, looking for a crack in their security. It was tedious, but worth the effort. Finally, he found a small hole he could exploit. He had limited access to the system but was able to see internal reports and daily receipts. It was a long way from carte blanche, but it was a start.

"Leia!"

She looked up, startled by his outburst.

"I found the reason Hans wanted us to be careful. That cute little local bank has over $100 million on deposit."

"A hundred million dollars! That's the connection." Suddenly she was next to his chair, tugging his arm, practically jumping up and down; her excitement was contagious.

He stood and wrapped his arms around her, pulling her close. Her soft breasts pressed against his chest when she shifted forward. He intended a quick hug, but his intentions changed when his hands skimmed from her shoulders to find her waist. Anchoring her hips against his hardening shaft, he was lost. He could smell that same floral scent in her hair, and when her lips parted, he leaned in, his mouth fitting to hers.

She hesitated at the first touch of their lips. Eric slid a hand up her back, cradling her head, weaving his fingers through her dark silky tresses. He angled her head so when his tongue swept in, she could kiss him back.

Her soft moan encouraged him. Pulling her flush against his body, he feasted. His lips trailed down her neck to sample her delicate skin. She arched against him, and he returned to her mouth, his teeth teasing her full bottom lip before he savored the taste of her again. He was throbbing hard and eager for more of the woman he held in his arms.

Reluctantly he brushed a final soft kiss to her lips, slid his fingers from her hair, and pulled back from her. She blinked up at him, her lips pink from his teeth and her breath short. He tugged her cardigan back into place over her shoulder and smoothed a hand down her arm.

With wide eyes, Leia staggered back, a supporting hand coming to rest on the dining room table. She blinked a few times and refocused. She looked to be pulling herself together faster than he was. What the hell was he doing? Leia was his chance for redemption—the client who had a righteous cause. She wasn't supposed to make his heart pound or his pulse race. He dragged a hand down his face, took a deep breath, and sat back in his chair, willing his erection to subside.

"We need to go to Savannah," she said, moving to sit on the couch.

Her eyes were bright, glittering with excitement, but he couldn't tell if it was from their embrace or the thought of hunting her enemies.

"What? No, we aren't going to Savannah."

He wasn't sure if his lovely accountant's reaction made perfect sense or pissed him off. That kiss was earth-shattering. He was reeling, and she wanted to chase the money to Georgia.

"Okay, mister hacker. You're in the system. Can you get us more details on the money?" she challenged.

She was right that his access to the bank was limited, but walking into a bank lobby wasn't going to get them any more information. They were safe in DC. The FBI would figure out the Oblonsky file she left them was real any minute now; they had some competent people at the agency. She should stay close to Simms.

"No. But that isn't necessary; that's the FBI's job. We'll give the info to Simms."

"Now you think the FBI can handle this? Then why am I writing a fifty-page report explaining Sal's methods?" She crossed her arms over her chest and glared at him.

"To get them to protect you."

"Because you don't want to babysit me anymore?"

"I didn't say that. I don't think that." Eric's stomach lurched at the thought of leaving Leia under the protection of the mindless law enforcement drones he'd seen at the FBI headquarters. "I don't have the FBI's resources. Once they have the report, you have more options." He was losing control of this conversation. He wanted to protect her, help her get the justice she was looking for, but he wouldn't risk her safety. Killing Max to save another person's life had altered him, but if he failed Leia and she died because of his mistake—he didn't even want to think about that kind of guilt.

"I can't finish the report if I don't understand what's happening in that bank in Savannah," she shot back.

"What are you going to learn standing in a bank lobby? It's not like they'll hand you their computer files. We're safe here. If we're moving, we could make a mistake, or Max could get lucky and find us. We need a good defense, and right now that is this apartment."

"You can help me stop them. We can do this together." She looked so earnest.

Exasperated, he exhaled loudly. "I will help you the best way I know how, by keeping you safe."

He wanted to be her savior, help her hunt them down, but never at the risk of her life.

"My dad always said a good offense is the best defense."

"Don't. No sports analogies. This location is perfect. We're safe and close to Agent Simms for when he finally calls. Get back to work on your report. I'll call for some dinner." He turned his back on the woman that had him both more frustrated and more aroused than he thought possible.

If he didn't find his cell and order food, he would be pinning Leia to a wall and kissing her until she melted at his feet and forgot all about an impromptu trip to Savannah. This apartment was a bunker, and they had no reason to leave.

Fuming, Leia stomped over to get her computer, fished out a pair of earbuds, and plugged them into the side of the laptop. The hum of angry music came from the direction of the couch; Eric tried not to roll his eyes. Hopefully, the pizza place could deliver a case of beer. It looked like it was going to be a long night.

EIGHT

SHE SLEPT LIKE SHIT. Sharing an overwhelming kiss and then arguing with the man who'd chosen to protect her from a bunch of gangsters was bad enough. Add half a greasy pizza, and it was the perfect recipe for nightmares and indigestion. Memories of Max busting into the hotel room morphed into dreams of him kicking down the door to their garden apartment refuge. Every time she would fall asleep, a more lurid and violent version of the nightmare would play in her head.

She yearned for coffee this morning with a white-hot passion. That it was six a.m. wasn't going to stop her. She crept down the hall in the near darkness, not wanting to wake up Eric. It was early; if he was still asleep, it was only fair to let him stay that way.

In the back of her mind, she had to admit that she was hiding from him. Operating in stealth mode to avoid an awkward conversation. She'd been pushing to go to Savannah without thinking about consequences. She might have to apologize. Ugh, she hated that. Yes, best to let sleeping dogs, or in this case man, lie.

Leia glanced at the couch to make sure Eric was still asleep, and she halted. He was shirtless, the blanket tangled over his lower body, one arm tossed over his head. Heat bloomed across her face. His well-defined upper body was a study in light and shadow, each dip hidden in darkness and every ridge illuminated by the early morning sunlight slanting in the small window. The light sprinkling of dark chest hair made her want to press her breasts into him, feel it against her peaked nipples. The memory of yesterday's kiss echoed, her lips tingled, desire heated her blood.

That man was dangerously good looking in a suit, but mostly naked he would rob any woman of her common sense. That he'd kissed her, touched her, and then carried her to bed the other night was more exciting than anything that had happened on her last three internet dates combined. Dry spell did not begin to explain her recent dating history; it was like the Sahara during global warming.

On an exhale, she restarted her journey to the kitchen, concentrating on her goal: coffee. She took one more glance at sleeping Eric, his gorgeous chest rising and falling in a regular rhythm, his handsome face soft and relaxed. Leia wasn't paying attention when she slammed into one of the dining room chairs, knocking it to the floor. Mortified, she dove for the ladderback chair to set it to rights, her face flaming hot. If he woke up and realized his naked chest was a weapon, he might never put a shirt on again.

The loud crash had Eric springing up from the couch, throwing off his blanket, and pulling a small handgun from somewhere. He turned toward the door first, then swiveled to Leia, his chest rising and falling rapidly as he searched for a threat. She stared unabashedly at him, and her face glowed even hotter. Skimpy navy boxer briefs outlined every hard inch of his cock, the thin fabric clinging like a second skin. They both paused. Eric lowered the gun and lifted one eyebrow, a taunting smile curving his very talented lips when he realized where her eyes were focused.

"Sorry, I'm...I was, I wanted—ah cocky, I mean coffee."

Did she *really* just say that? Kissing him yesterday must have fried a few brain cells. She flipped around, hiding her supernova level blush from him, and beelined for the coffee pot.

"Oh, fuck my life," she mumbled under her breath. It was an honest slip of the tongue when ambushed by Eric's morning glory. If the floor could open and swallow her right now, it would be ideal.

Fumbling with the coffee filters, Leia tried to will away her blush; it felt permanent. A cold shower might be able to douse the flames. She dumped a heap of coffee grounds into the top of the machine. This may be the worst coffee in the history of the District of Colombia, but caffeine was the only thing that might get her through the morning without self-combusting or climbing Eric like a tree.

Yesterday's kiss was a revelation. She'd melted into a puddle of need so quickly. He was some kind of sorcerer. When released from his embrace, her brain short-circuited and fixated on the first PG-rated topic she could think of: the bank in Savannah. A kiss like that this morning, and Leia would be peeling those briefs off him with her teeth.

She knew she could trust Eric to protect her; he already proved that when Max broke down the hotel room door. But falling into bed with a guy that admits to living most of his life on the wrong side of the law was different. Kissing him was a temptation she'd be wise to resist.

"Need some help?" Eric stood behind her, his arms caging her against the kitchen counter while he drawled his question into her ear. He nuzzled his cheek against her, his morning scruff abrading her neck, but otherwise, he didn't touch her. All she needed to do was lean back, and she would be flush against the body she was just ogling, sealed against him from chest to hips. She was sure even her toes were blushing.

"Help?" she squeaked.

"Aren't we making coffee?"

"Water?" Leia struggled to remove the pot and slide it next to his hand, which was resting on the counter. He had great hands; they looked capable. Her arm movement pushed her elbow against his taut abs. She almost moaned at the contact.

"Your wish is my desire," he purred, his lips brushing the shell of her ear as they moved to form the words.

Her flushed skin tingled from his breath. Then he was gone, pushing back from the counter with the coffee pot in hand, strolling over to the sink to fill it. Leia was trying to decide between crying in embarrassment and wanting to kiss the smirk from his lips.

A loud ding from the burner phone sounded from the coffee table. He set the water-filled pot on the counter, leaving it behind to retrieve the phone. His sexy swagger dissolved when he started reading and replying to the text messages lighting up his cell.

She finished pouring the water into the machine and switched the coffee on to brew, waiting for him to look up from his phone. His expression was focused. Whoever he was texting with wasn't giving him good news.

"Katherine will be stopping by in a few hours; we should get cleaned up so we can both hear what she has to say," he said without looking up from the phone.

"I'll take the first shower." Her strained voice sounded funny to her ears. She was thrilled to have a reason to put some distance between herself and Eric.

He looked up. "You need any help? I can scrub your back." His sexy smirk had reappeared.

Leia scampered for the bedroom and a cold shower at full speed. Coffee would have to wait.

She showered and dressed in yesterday's jeans and a slouchy sweater. Sitting on the bathroom counter, she used the only decent light in the back half of the apartment to put on a touch of makeup. Between the smoldering looks she and Eric kept tossing around and the impending arrival of the mysterious Katherine, a bit of war paint seemed like a good idea. Happy with her makeup, she headed back out to the living area to let Eric know he could have the bathroom. Hopefully, the coffee was drinkable.

He pressed a full cup of black coffee into her hands as soon as she stepped into the little kitchen area. Smiling a thank-you, she met his gaze. He'd put on a pair of jeans and a shirt. With less manly skin on display Leia thought she could string together coherent sentences that didn't include references to any part of the male anatomy.

"I should apologize," Eric started.

"For what?"

"This morning."

"Which part of this morning? The part where you did a *Magic Mike* impression with a gun?"

He chuckled into his coffee cup. "Ah, no, but nice to know my vigilance was appreciated. No, the part where I embarrassed you."

"Nope! If you apologize for that, I have to apologize for pouting last night." Leia wanted to get any kind of apologies over with quickly and with the least fuss possible; they always made her squirm.

Eric bravely soldiered on. "You were just so tempting this morning, that blush... I wanted to see how red I could make you. I am sorry about that. It wasn't my finest moment, but I like knowing I can affect you."

He was leaning against the countertop, watching Leia, looking for another blush probably. She waved her hand dismissively; she didn't want this apology. If he knew she'd been gawking at his body when she tripped on the chair, he would know there was no reason to apologize.

"My turn. When I get angry or flustered, I kind of shut down. My dad called it pouting. Good news is I don't yell or throw things when I'm mad. Bad news—in the moment, I'm unable to have a meaningful conversation about anything. I fixated on Georgia as the answer to all my problems, and when you said no, I zoned out." She was happy to have this conversation over; she sipped her coffee to cover the pause in the conversation. "The bathroom is all yours."

He pushed away from the counter and deposited his coffee mug in the sink before looking back at her as he headed for the bedroom hallway. "As long as no one is sorry about that kiss." Before rounding the corner into the hall, he tossed a smoldering wink over his shoulder at her.

Playful, sexy Eric was swoon-worthy. Her stomach clenched, her face flushed, and she wanted another of his kisses. The memory of him nearly naked with a gun flashed in her mind. She might never have fallen for the big strong protector type in the past, but being in real danger made the appeal clear.

NINE

KATHERINE FORD WAS the kind of woman men conjured up in their dreams; she had curves like Marilyn Monroe, skin like fine porcelain, and mahogany hair that glittered in the sun. She was also one of the few people Eric trusted enough to ask for help. He'd met her at a low point in her life, helping to clean up a mistake that could have destroyed Katherine's world. She was ruthless but loyal to her allies.

Katherine breezed into the garden apartment in a cloud of expensive perfume, using her key to get inside. Dressed in a low-cut sage green Escada suit and taupe four-inch Prada heels, she personified business elegant. Her manicured hands gripped an overflowing take-out bag emblazoned with the logo of the Blue Duck Tavern, the favorite breakfast spot for DC's see-and-be-seen crowd, in one hand and a Hermes purse in the other.

It would be hard to guess Katherine was a poor relation in her family. She was one of those Fords, the automobile company type. But her father was a scapegrace cousin who pissed away every dime he had long before his beautiful daughter was born. The money and influence Katherine had was her own. Early on, she learned men underestimated her intelligence, and she'd taken that to the bank.

"Eric, so wonderful to see you outside New York; that city is such a cesspool." Katherine leaned in to give him a lingering, one-armed embrace.

He concluded years ago that Katherine's sexual relationships most closely resembled those of the praying mantis. Metaphorically speaking, she was capable of biting a lover's head off and devouring his corpse for nourishment. Eric was happy to keep his head attached to his body, so they had been *only* friends since he did his first job for her eight years ago.

"Katherine, you live in DC. Doesn't the rest of our nation refer to this city as The Swamp?" Eric replied.

"Touché, but it's my swamp." She looked toward Leia, who was seated at the dining room table with her laptop. A knowing look appeared on Katherine's face. "I see why you were willing to journey to my fair city."

Katherine strolled to the table, placing the take-out bag down and reaching one slim hand out to Leia. "I am Katherine Ford. Don't believe half of what Eric has told you about me. It's all well thought out lies to keep my image intact."

Leia took the proffered hand in hers, looking up at Katherine a little dazed. "He hasn't told me a thing."

"That is just like a man. We can chat over breakfast."

Eric couldn't imagine what Leia thought of Katherine with her calculating eyes and thousand-dollar shoes.

Katherine began to unpack a buffet of waffles, breakfast sandwiches, and fresh fruit while peppering Leia with questions. Eric was sure the food would taste even better than it looked and smelled. Katherine was a true hedonist in every sense of the word. Good food, great wine, and gorgeous lovers.

"Eric, she's a CPA, too smart for you." Katherine laughed at her final determination.

Katherine's interrogation of Leia had been harmless, and Leia held her own. He was impressed. Leia must be accustomed to the Park Avenue vultures in New York; he would have to ask her what she thought of Katherine in comparison.

"Thank you for the concern, Katherine. I shall endeavor to keep up with her."

He shot a private smile to Leia, one she returned. When their eyes met, a spark flared between them that pushed his pulse a beat faster.

The contrast between the two women was evident. Katherine oozed confidence and cynicism while Leia was more genuine and unassuming, but they were equals in mental agility. He was surprised to feel pride swelling in his chest, unaware he'd developed a vested interest in how others perceived Leia.

Katherine would hold any critical information she had to share until their meal was over; it was just her way. Never ruin a delicious meal with bad news. The fact she hadn't included mimosas in their brunch did concern him that her information would be significant.

The food cleared away and a final round of coffees poured, Katherine began.

"Eric, when I texted this morning, I told you not to send out for food or answer the door for a good reason. An SUV of dangerous looking men is waiting for someone to emerge from the Australian Embassy. They arrived some-time late yesterday and have staked out the block since. I assume these men think you two are inside?"

Eric rubbed a palm over the back of his neck sheepishly admitting, "I might have hacked into the Aussie's Wi-Fi. The laptops were running a cloaking program, but with enough time and money, someone could have traced the IP address back to the embassy. I figured on a few more days before they would unravel it."

"Marcus, the ambassador, had security run the New Jersey plates on the SUV; they traced back to some holding company in Hoboken. He asked if I wanted to handle it or if his security guys should. Eric, I fear my building isn't going to keep you safe much longer, even with the ambassador living above you. I think relocating and leaving your friends from New Jersey behind would be for the best."

"I agree. More than one guy?"

Katherine nodded.

"Do you think it's Max?" Leia asked, fear in her eyes.

"Isn't Max dead?" Katherine looked confused.

"Max appears to be back from the dead. He always worked alone. I would say this is a different crew," Eric informed her.

Getting up from the table, he paced the small room. At the narrow window near the door, he tried to look out, but from the basement viewpoint, all he could see were tires, feet, and curbs. They needed a new plan.

Leia wanted to visit the bank in Savannah; it might be a good time to grant her wish. The drive down I-95 would be only a few hours, and Savannah was a great city to get lost in with tourists and college kids filling the streets day and night. He even had a few connections outside the city.

Putting eight hundred miles between them and New York would help ensure their safety. As long as they used cash and were smart, they could disappear.

"Leia, want to see what St Patrick's Day is like in Savannah?" he asked.

⊗

"SAVANNAH IT IS. We'll need a distraction and a car; I don't want to risk taking the rental that's in my name," Eric said.

"I can help with both." Katherine pulled Leia back toward the bedroom hall, waving goodbye with jazz fingers at Eric. Katherine's excitement was palpable; Leia was sure that she was about to be dragged out of her comfort zone.

Leia didn't expect a glamorous creature like Katherine to giggle, but when she tucked Leia under her arm to pull her toward the dark bedroom, she was laughing like a twelve-year-old having a sleepover.

"We need a costume change!" Katherine plopped on the bed, toeing off her spectacular heels. "Before you pack your bag, do you have any workout clothes?"

Leia headed to her knapsack to start digging. She hadn't wrapped her mind around what exactly Katherine was to Eric: friend, client, or ex? Either way, Katherine was the kind of polished and perfect woman that Leia would see in Manhattan. They were the apex predators of barrooms and board rooms, and it was best to stay out of their way. Having the undivided focus of this kind of woman was making her feel every inch the nerdy accountant she was.

Digging out a black sports bra, running leggings, and a fleece jacket, she presented them to Katherine, who snapped up the bra.

"Anything else small and short for the bottoms?"

Leia found the black sleep shorts she wore last night. "This what you want?"

"Perfect!" Katherine was practically jumping off the bed with glee.

Standing in front of the dresser mirror, Katherine

worked to take down her elaborate hairstyle. Leia gazed at their reflections. Comparing her appearance to the other woman, she felt a twinge of envy. Her dark brown hair seemed dull and her slim figure boyish in contrast to Katherine's red-headed pin-up model looks. Katherine and Eric would be a striking couple; she could envision them jetting to a luxury vacation or dining in a five-star restaurant.

"You are good for him," Katherine said, meeting Leia's gaze in the mirror, her fingers pulling the last few pins from her hair.

"No, it's not like that. He's just helping me."

"My dear, Eric hasn't done an altruistic thing in a decade." Planting her hands on her hips, she turned her laser-like gaze on Leia. "He never leaves the city of New York for a paying client. He barely leaves his home office for them, but you brought him to DC. When you move or speak, he watches. He's fascinated by you."

"I'm not that fascinating."

"You can demur all you like, but that tingle in the air when the two of you look at each other is real." Turning back to the mirror, Katherine shrugged out of her jacket. "Pass me that bra and shorts. My girls squeezed into your top... I'll be quite the distraction for the gentlemen from New Jersey."

Laughing, she walked into the bathroom to change. "This will be fun!"

The frivolous sparkle in Katherine's eyes was infectious. When she reappeared, Leia couldn't stop the laughter that bubbled out. The constrictive top and minuscule shorts were obscene on Katherine's lush figure. The acres of alabaster skin exposed both above and below the sports bra would distract any man.

"I know, isn't this great!" Katherine stalked the

bedroom in an exaggerated catlike stroll, swinging her hips and shimmying her shoulders. One shimmy too many, and she was fixing a wardrobe malfunction that sent them both into peals of laughter. Staring at her reflection, Katherine sobered for a moment and said, "I would only do something like this for one of two reasons. The first: money, lots of it. The second: Eric."

"You like him?" Leia felt a twinge of jealousy; she would never be able to compete for Eric's affections if Katherine wanted him.

"No worries, my dear. That ship sailed many years ago, and neither one of us was on board. Eric is like a brother to me, but far smarter and more useful than any man I'm related to."

Not sure how to reply to Katherine's assertion, Leia said, "You might cause a riot if you go outside like that."

"Don't worry. On this street, I am a queen." Katherine executed the royal wave with an exaggerated flourish, nodding her head to imaginary subjects.

"This building has been mine for a few years, and every Australian ambassador for a generation has rented it. The current ambassador, Marcus, is darling and a passably attentive lover. The thugs from New Jersey have no idea, but if they get too close to me, I have an entire barracks of large angry Aussie guards with diplomatic immunity happy to defend me."

Leia nodded in understanding but honestly couldn't imagine ever calling herself a queen in any situation, though it was evident Katherine relished the position. "Shall we go show Eric your outfit?"

Carrying Katherine's unneeded designer clothes, they emerged to find Eric bent over a laptop in the main room. Leia wished she still had her phone. His double-take when confronted with Katherine's cleavage would've been video gold.

"You'll freeze. It's March," he pointed out when he was capable of forming a coherent sentence.

"Ha, I'm just going around the block." Katherine pulled a pair of running shoes from the depths of her over-sized Birkin bag. "You two are going out the window. Across the alley, you'll find my navy Jaguar. Eric, she is new, be kind to her." Katherine tossed a key fob in his direction.

Catching the key, he asked, "What window? How is this place legal to rent as an apartment? There's no fire exit."

The apartment windows were all high up the walls and small. Eric was a decent size guy over six feet tall with broad shoulders. Leia couldn't see this working.

"Such little faith. You will fit. At least that's what the building department seems to think. The bedroom has the biggest window, but it's visible from the street, so I'll need to make sure the boys from Jersey are as taken with my appearance as you were." Katherine slid her hands down her body, highlighting her bountiful assets.

THIS WAS the most fun he ever had escaping a basement. Strictly speaking, he'd never escaped a basement before, but getting this front-row view to Leia's firm ass in those skinny jeans would make any activity entertaining.

"Are you certain you don't want to go first?" she asked before she levered the tiny window open. Standing on her tippy toes atop the rickety dresser, she was just able to open the latch and swing the pane wide. She shoved their hastily packed bags out the window and off to one side of the opening.

"Yep." Eric popped the "P" at the end of the word. Standing below her, he was getting ready to help boost Leia out the window. His fingers were already tingling at the thought of getting ahold of her butt.

"Just hook your arms on the windowsill, and I'll help you out," he told her.

Leia hoisted herself up on the window ledge. Eric stepped onto the dresser behind her, grabbed two handfuls of her succulent ass, and pushed her out to the street level. The adorable gasp when he grabbed her cheeks made him wish he could savor the process a bit more.

The way her eyes had devoured every inch of his near-naked body this morning had him eager for a reason to touch her. She may look young and innocent, but this morning, she was all desire and need. He was ready to see where that could lead; good intentions be damned. Hiding in Savannah seemed like the perfect situation for exploring their attraction.

With a grunt and a few curses, Leia was out the window; now it was his turn. Pulling himself up was simple enough. The undignified wiggling that was needed to wedge his shoulders out the window left Leia suppressing a giggle.

Finally, he rolled over, flat on his back in the side yard of the Ambassador's residence. Tipping his head to his right and looking down the alley, he could see Katherine using a sidewalk flower planter to do a hamstring stretch. She was a car length in front of a black SUV that must have the boys from New Jersey in it. They would be getting an eyeful.

Katherine dared a look in their direction before changing to an erotic shoulder exercise; the spandex sports bra was fighting a valiant battle to contain her bountiful chest. If she sneezed, everything would pop free. Eric wished he could stay to see the entire show.

Getting up from the ground, he toed the basement window closed. How he fit through that he didn't know. Leia had turned to gape at the performance that Katherine was putting on. And what a performance it was.

"Leia, head for the parking lot. Stay in front of me." Using his body to obstruct the view of the guys in the SUV, Eric carried their bags in one hand and fished Katherine's car key out of his pocket with the other.

Daring a glance over his shoulder, he almost choked, Katherine was doing something up against a small maple tree planted along the sidewalk that would have earned a stripper a twenty-dollar tip. A parade of elephants could march down Massachusetts Avenue and those guys wouldn't notice.

Surrounded by a chain-link fence, the Embassy's visitor parking lot was a short walk from the window they crawled out. They slipped in through a small gate on the alleyway, and Eric clicked the key fob.

Oh, yeah! The midnight blue two-door Jaguar F-Type sat in a sea of eco-friendly commuter cars and boring SUVs. Its massive rear tires and matching chrome twin exhaust pipes screamed race car; Eric couldn't wait to get it on the highway.

He opened the passenger door for Leia. "My lady." He seated her in the car with a flourish. The bags safely tucked in the trunk, he got behind the wheel. The purr of the oversized engine was glorious; the luxury interior smelled like money and felt like butter.

"I'll have to tell Katherine I approve of her choice of vehicles." Sliding out of the parking spot, he pulled down the alley and toward Massachusetts Avenue.

"Oh my!" Leia pointed and laughed as she looked at the chaos across the street.

Wrapped in the jacket and beefy arms of one of the embassy guards, Katherine stood to one side, chatting with a police officer. The officer was trying his best to direct his conversation to Katherine's face, but the gap in the front of the guard's jacket was the perfect frame for Katherine's spectacular cleavage.

Another officer was looking at the damage to the black SUV, where a gray sedan had sideswiped it. The driver of the car was a middle-aged guy in a cheap wrinkled suit. He was on the sidewalk with two of the hired thugs, wringing his hands and gesturing toward Katherine. The Jersey guys looked nervous, but that might be because of the telltale bulge of handguns Eric could see under their black suit coats.

"I told her she would freeze to death." Eric guided the Jag past the carnage and headed for southbound Interstate 95.

DRIVING HAD ALWAYS HELPED Eric clear his mind, and the responsive Jag made it even better. In New York, he had a vintage Porsche he took for weekend drives. He loved the old manual transmission and gritty power of the car, but this Jag was pretty fabulous.

Leia was good company in the car. Her music taste was even more eclectic than his, and she knew the words to just about every song they had agreed on listening to. Her voice had a lovely husky quality that made him think of chocolate and bourbon. She'd fallen asleep about twenty miles ago, four hours into the eight-hour drive. With her eyes closed, he could see the dark spikes of her long lashes against the cream skin of her cheeks. Listening to her soft breathing while he drove was strangely intimate. It stirred something in him he wasn't sure he'd felt in years.

Getting out of DC undetected had lifted a weight off his shoulders that he'd been carrying since the DC hotel attack. If Max Davenport and that crew from Jersey were after Leia, Sal Marino must have put a considerable price tag on her life. The good news was that Savannah was busting at the seams with tourists coming in for the St Patrick's Day festivities. The overcrowded city would be perfect camouflage, allowing them to hide in plain sight.

Eric was more concerned that Max was after them than anyone else. Max was resourceful, deadly, and wanted revenge, but something about him had seemed wrong. Leia had called Max psycho, and Eric was inclined to agree. Max had always been a cold, calculating soldier. The wild-eyed attacker in the hotel didn't line up with the man Eric worked with for five years. In the heat of the moment, Eric ignored the changes in Max to focus on the fight, but with time to reflect, he felt like Max was off his game.

He had connected with Max during the months leading up to his application to the FBI training program at Quantico. They were both completing their applications and had struck up a virtual friendship in an FBI related chat room. Eric was a computer nerd with jock tendencies, Max an ex-marine who wanted to keep serving his country but do it stateside. They received their FBI rejection letters on the same day; online venting led to meeting in real life. Their work as fixers had started as the natural blending of their respective talents.

As the miles of highway slipped away, Eric thought about the night everything had come crashing down. It was a straightforward job, going to a mistress's house to destroy any evidence of her relationship with their client.

The client was getting ready to run for national political office, and a twenty-two-year-old mistress didn't mesh with his family values image. After destroying all the evidence, they were to take her to a private plane that was on standby to fly her home to her mother in South America. The aspiring politico was betting her lack of legal immigration status would keep her out of his way.

He and Max were to destroy her computers, diaries, and even her cell phone. Often for this kind of job, Max would handle all the fieldwork, and Eric would do everything he needed via the internet. They had teamed up that night because Eric wanted to get on the girl's computer. Her cybersecurity was top-notch, and she'd avoided all his phishing emails so he couldn't get into her system remotely. He needed to sit in front of her actual system.

He and Max had gotten into the girl's apartment easily as her lover had supplied them with a key and the alarm code. Eric recalled how terrified she was, screaming at them in Spanish, trying to run. Eric tried to reason with her, to explain if she calmed down and cooperated, it would all be fine.

Max barreled past him and grabbed the frightened girl. He had her zip-tied to a kitchen chair in seconds with a gag tied firmly around her head. Her tears ruined her mascara, the wet tracks running down her cheeks, staining the gag along the edge.

He recalled how her muffled sobs had echoed in the small apartment as he sat at her computer, working through all the files and online accounts and erasing everything. And he remembered how Max never glanced at the girl after he'd tied her up, seemingly immune to her tears. Max worked methodically, going from room to room, searching for physical evidence, building a pile of papers and photos that he would torch.

Once Eric had finished with the computer, he went into the kitchen and started to speak with the girl, figuring it would be much simpler to get her to the airport if she was calm. Max ignored them while burning all the paper evidence of the want-to-be Senator's affair in the kitchen sink. When he finished, he pulled out a black zipper bag. The small bag looked innocent enough, only a little bigger than Max's palm. At the time, Eric hadn't understood what he was seeing, but he'd had five years to understand and to replay it over and over in his mind.

Max set a hypodermic needle on the kitchen counter along with a small unlabeled vial.

"What is that?" Eric asked.

Max never looked at him, never faltered, just kept working to ready the needle with quiet speed and precision.

Max cruelly twisted the young woman's left arm up, exposing her veins. His eyes were dilated, his skin flushed and breathing erratic in some strange state of heightened arousal. The needle was steady in Max's hand, poised above the woman's skin.

Eric snapped out of his confusion and slapped the hypodermic out of Max's grasp; it spun almost in slow motion, the sharp point glistening in the bright kitchen lights, before it felt to the hard tile floor and rolled away.

"What's in the fucking syringe?" Eric asked again, his hand shackled around Max's wrist.

"Heroin. I'm making a bonus on this evening's work. Now get the hell out of my way." He tugged free of Eric's grip.

The girl was in hysterics, hyperventilating behind the gag and frantically against the plastic ties that held her to the chair.

"We don't kill people. We're the alternative, fast and

quiet. We get rid of problems but keep our client's hands clean. That's always been our objective."

Eric clenched his fists, digging his nails into palms. This wasn't how they operated. The moment Max had unzipped that black bag, he'd ended their partnership.

"Fuck the objective! I want the money. Money we could have been making together if you weren't so stupid." Max scanned the kitchen floor for the syringe. "The best way to fix a problem like her is to kill her. So, I got in touch with the soon to be senator and worked a side deal. There's no airplane waiting to take her home to whatever godforsaken country she was born in. There's just me and that needle."

Eric still wasn't sure who threw the first punch. His recollection of the fight was a blur, but his injuries testified that it was vicious. The distortion becomes crystal clear at the point when he wrapped his fingers around Max's neck. Even now, the feeling of Max's pulse, at first erratic, then beginning to slow, was vivid in his mind, along with the way his breath choked and sputtered until it finally stopped. But it was Max's rage-filled eyes blinking against the pain until they ultimately slipped closed that haunted Eric's dreams. Squeezing the life out of his partner's body, of the moment he became a killer—or so he thought—was etched clearly in his memory.

Eric flexed his fingers on the smooth leather of the Jag's steering wheel, bringing himself back to the present. Looking at Leia, he thought about why he didn't tell her he killed Max. In part, it was shame; she wouldn't look at him the same once she knew he was a killer. Having her trust was necessary to keep her safe. In part he was still trying to understand what happened. Max was alive, and yet Eric knew he'd killed him. He'd checked for a pulse. That Max was alive didn't magically erase the guilt he'd carried for years over killing his partner.

Explaining the convoluted truth to her after she'd just survived Max's attack on the hotel room wouldn't have helped anything. He should've told her at the safe house, but now it was a festering half lie that he didn't want to face. Leia was finally relaxing and accepting that he wanted to help her. Her trust was a fragile thing, and he wouldn't do anything to undermine that.

If she didn't trust him, he couldn't protect her. She would second-guess his motives, and second-guessing in a crisis could be fatal.

Leia stretched in the seat next to him, waking up slowly.

"You want to stop? We can grab a coffee and something to eat," Eric offered.

"Sure. Sounds like a plan."

TEN

THE SAVANNAH CARRIAGE house had the tiniest garage she'd ever seen; it was on the alleyway off the main street. The arched opening had a vintage barn door secured with a digital lock. Once open, it was easy to tell the garage was a horse's stall at one time. Watching Eric shoehorn the glistening Jaguar into the narrow opening made Leia happy she wasn't driving.

While he finished parking, she used another code to open the blue front door. Inside it was like a dollhouse.

"Eric, this place is adorable. Can we stay forever?" she called to him.

Leia was charmed. The carriage house that Eric had rented using a fake identity on a vacation rental website was tucked in behind a stately three-story Savannah row house on an oak-lined street close to Forsyth Park.

"I don't think the owners of the big house are planning on letting us stay longer than the two weeks I booked," he replied while locking the front door.

"How did you get this house with everyone in town for St Patrick's Day?"

Apparently, Savannah did St Pat's like New Orleans did Mardi Gras. In the city squares, even the water in the fountains had been dyed green. Tuesday was the big parade. She was pretty sure somewhere on her dad's side of the family she was Irish enough to enjoy a green beer.

"Just lucky, I guess." He was just a bit red across his cheekbones and wouldn't meet her gaze. Bashful or embarrassed, it was hard to tell. Either way, it was endearing.

"Eric? How much did this place cost?" She had an idea his flush was because she was going to be astonished at how much he'd spent keeping her safe.

"So about that, it's not a money thing. It's about safety. We need privacy and a garage, and in the right neighbor-hood. This house has all that and an alarm system." He ticked off the items on one hand before he scooped up the bags.

Downstairs there was a mile of chintz drapes, eques-trian-themed art on every wall, and a tastefully curated collection of antique furniture. In the cozy living area, the original floors, scarred and gouged, had been polished and stained a rich walnut. Under an impossibly steep staircase, there was a small but fully appointed kitchen with reclaimed furniture as cabinets and new stainless steel appliances. The white plaster ceiling showed off the wide wood beams that supported the second floor, which Leia assumed had been a hayloft.

"I'll just put our bags in the bedroom." Eric had to duck under at least one of the massive beams to make it up the stairs. He was avoiding the money conversation.

Leia decided that the staircase was either charming or a death trap, which might depend on the time of night or number of cocktails you'd had before your climb. It had two landings, uneven treads, and was so narrow Eric had to put one bag in front of him and twist his other arm behind him with the second bag.

"*The* bedroom?" Leia asked as she followed.

"It was a compromise. If I wanted a place that had a second bed, we would've either been in a hotel suite or an unacceptable neighborhood."

"This sounds like New York City real estate. How much?" She waited while they navigated the stairs.

"I've stayed at a five-star hotel in Paris for less," he admitted when he reached the top.

The upstairs bedroom was a dream. A king-sized four-poster bed with intricate carvings and white gauze hangings dominated the room, the finials on top of the posts almost touching the vaulted ceiling. Leia had no idea how the bed or mattress made it up those stairs, but not her problem. She was happy to enjoy the fruits of an interior decorator's struggles. The room felt like it belonged in a posh southern hunting lodge. Fox hunting scenes decorated the walls and wooden duck decoys were used as knick-knacks. More of the original hardwoods gleamed under her feet, and through a door, she could see a claw foot tub. Sumptuous velvet drapes framed the window that over-looked the brick courtyard between the carriage house and the main home.

"Oh, I love it up here. Worth whatever you paid. I will pay you back, you know." She meant it, too. The idea of him shouldering all the expenses didn't sit well with her. She was already in debt to him for saving her life; she could come up with some money toward their accommo-dations. As soon as she could access her bank account, she'd take care of it.

Leia hurried across the room to open the other closed doors like it was Christmas morning. She found a brand-new washer and dryer in a well-appointed laundry room and a large walk-in closet. "Laundry, ah, I have never been so happy to see a washer and dryer."

"I'll bunk on the, uh, whatever that is." Eric pointed at a ladies fainting couch that sat in a corner, upholstered in tufted toile fabric complete with dark blue fringe on the skirt. The delicate item would never accommodate his size.

"It's a fainting couch, and you won't sleep there because you can't. It's too small for you. I'll take the fainting couch, and the first shower," she told him.

"That couch thing looked bigger in the web photos," he grumbled. He headed for the stairs. "I'll call and get us some dinner. Any requests?"

"Surprise me."

Leia was thrilled to grab a shower after a day on the road. Before she stripped she'd piled her laundry on the floor, ready to go in the machine, leaving out just what she planned to wear.

The hot water pounded on her stiff muscles helping chase away the knots from sitting in the car. The bathroom had been fully stocked with fluffy towels and fancy bath products. While the expensive conditioner soaked into her hair, she let her mind wander to Eric. His long fingers wrapped around the Jag's steering wheel. Thick forearms with just a sprinkling of manly hair. She shifted her thighs together, thoughts like these only led one place. She almost reached for the handheld massage shower head on the wall. If she went there while thinking of him she'd never again be able to look him in the eyes without blushing. She stifled a frustrated groan. The man was such eye candy. She tipped her head into the hot spray and rinsed the conditioner out. Maybe a cold shower would have been a better idea.

Wrapped in a towel with her wet hair in a turban on her head, she bent over to pile her clothes into the washing machine. As she was shoving in her last pair of jeans, she heard Eric's footsteps. When she turned, he was behind her leaning one shoulder against the doorjamb. She was confident she'd just caught him checking out her ass. The tiny towel she was wrapped in barely covered her. Her face flushed with a mix of embarrassment and a zing of arousal. Her naughty thoughts from the shower came back full force. A cold shower would definitely have been smart.

"So we aren't getting anything delivered," he told her, his eyes lingering on her naked legs. "We can try for take-out, but even that sounds like a long shot. The population of the city doubles for the St Pat's weekend, and the restaurants are slammed. We have to go out, find a restaurant, or a grocery." He ran a frustrated hand over his face, finally dragging his eyes up from her legs to meet her gaze.

"Uhh, so we get to go out?" Leia loved this, as much as she knew staying in was smart and what Eric had originally planned. She really wanted to see some of the city.

"Yes, but just for food. I don't want to leave you here alone. Bring a jacket, it might get chilly. And be sure you can walk in your shoes."

"So, it's a date?"

"Just put some clothes on," he growled back, looking like he was thinking about tugging her towel off and staying home.

Eric's eyes darkened with desire. She gripped the top of her towel tighter and moved to slip past him and out of the laundry room. He reached out, catching her jaw and tilting her head up to look at him. Leia's heart raced, and she instinctively leaned into his touch. Goosebumps rose on her naked arms.

"Yes, it's a date," he informed her. And with that pronouncement, he released her face and turned on his heel and headed back toward the stairs.

She sagged against the wall, letting out a big exhale. She could feel the imprint of his hand on her cheek. Her lips tingled, hungry for the kiss he hadn't given. Falling for your fixer had to be a bad idea, but the way her body felt right now, there was no way she was going to stop it.

THE MARCH EVENING air was crisp but pleasant, Eric took Leia's hand in his and started walking from the carriage house toward one of Savannah's quaint city squares. There was just enough daylight left to indulge in a bit of sightseeing on their way to the main downtown area where the restaurants were located.

"Have you ever been to Savannah before?" he asked. He scanned the streets, looking for anything out of place.

"No, but a few years ago, I read the book about the famous murder in Mercer house."

"Sure, I think the house is a few blocks the other way." Eric gestured behind them.

Leia was busy soaking up the atmosphere, her eyes darting from the brick streets lined with oak trees, to the Gaelic decorations tied to the wrought iron railings on the row houses. He appreciated seeing the city through her eyes. When he'd been here in the past, it was for business, not pleasure.

A particularly stately home with a beautiful side yard caught her attention. She grabbed his hand, interlacing their fingers and pulling him across the street. She leaned against the intricate wrought iron gate to admire the private garden.

He glanced down at their interlaced hands; her small hand felt delicate wrapped around his. It surprised him how natural it felt. It wasn't just holding her hand, but spending time with her was easy. They'd been cooped up for days together, and he wanted more of her, not less. He stepped closer, letting his arm brush her side. She turned and smiled at him.

She wore slick black leggings that clung to her spectacular legs and a soft sweater with an open neck that would slip low, giving him a tantalizing view of something lace she had on under it. Her practical low-heeled boots clicked on the uneven sidewalk, and on one arm, she'd draped the same black coat she had been wearing since DC.

She was unlike the women he was usually with; they wore Prada and Gucci like armor, the labels their best defense against the world. In her work clothing, Leia looked like a girl playing dress-up. But in her everyday clothes, she was tempting, a mixture of sex and innocence —the shoulder-baring sweater hinting at the beauty underneath, and her tight pants showing off her willowy curves.

Once Katherine had told them DC was compromised, he welcomed the move to Savannah. With eight hours of highway between them and Sal's goons, he felt like they could relax their guard a little. It would be good for them both to get out, walking the city after days cooped up in the DC apartment and the car.

He led her across Madison Square, stopping in front of the giant military statue in the center of the park. Someone had festooned the dignified soldier with a *"kiss me I'm Irish"* sash.

Their hands still clasped, she'd settled in close beside him, the scent of her shampoo teased him. Together they studied the statue.

"Poor guy, all dressed up, no place to go," she said.

"The least they could have done was bring him a beer."

Her eyes sparkled with laughter. She was so tempting in

that moment that he couldn't help himself. He wrapped a hand around her shoulder and turned her body so their lips met. His lips were firm, tasting her. He didn't rush, lingering to sample her mouth, his hand caressing her face. Leia leaned into him, pressing her body into his. A whimper slipped from her when he pulled away. Her eyes fluttered open, and she licked her lips. He restrained himself from tugging her back for another kiss.

Their hands still clasped, Eric turned away from the statue and headed toward Liberty Street. The crowds of tourists and college kids from the Savannah College of Art and Design, SCAD, were out in force tonight, all of them going to the city's waterfront park where the St Patrick's Day Festival had been raging since midday.

He wanted no part of the madness that came with the huge festival, so he planned to keep them on this side of town. He hoped a stack of cash would encourage one of the restaurants to find them a table. This was one of the busiest nights of the year in the city.

Turning the corner, he spotted a restaurant that looked like a decent spot. The gastropub had opened its retractable glass walls and brought out space heaters so the street party atmosphere of St Patrick's Day poured inside without being overwhelming. A table inside against a wall would offer some safety, and the open walls offered easy escape routes.

"Let's try this place, see if I can work some magic." He directed Leia toward the front where a bedraggled host stood behind a small podium.

Eric palmed a few hundred dollar bills he'd put in his front pocket. Thankfully, Katherine had been happy to resupply his cash reserves before they left DC.

Leaning close to the man, he asked, "Any chance at a table?"

He covertly flashed the cash to the host. The man was in his twenties, and the three hundred bucks was enough to turn his head even on a crazy night.

The host pocketed the money. "Give me five. Would bar seating work?" The man gestured toward a couple at the end of the bar who were paying.

They were soon seated at the side of the bar, the white subway tile wall on Leia's right and Eric on her left. Their location thrilled Eric, they could see everything and be part of the action, but the wall and nearby booth protected them from the madness of the overcrowded space. It was a little cocoon with a window on the world.

Eric settled into his seat, having deposited their coats with the host. Leia and the bartender were talking about craft beers; she was selecting flights of the most outlandish brews for them to sample and laughing at her selections. It was the laugh that drew Eric in, just like in the square earlier. It was authentic and tempting. She pulled him close, including him in the conversation, and he lived in the moment.

THE RESTAURANT WAS PACKED. Leia loved it. There were people to watch, great food, better beers, and Eric. Things between them were new; their connection was tenuous but promising. Walking to dinner, she'd been aware of him. His strong hand wrapped around hers and how he kept her close. It was a mix of protectiveness and attention that had her stomach in knots—the good kind. And that kiss in the square had left her wanting more.

"So, why did you change your mind about us coming to Savannah?" she asked after the server cleared away their appetizer plates.

"Do you want the strategic answer or the real reason?"

"Both please."

"Strategically, we're a decent distance from DC and a long way from New York, and I have some contacts outside the city if we need to run. There's an FBI field office, and the St. Patrick's Day madness is good cover."

"And the real reason?"

"I wanted to do something for you. So Monday we're visiting Savannah Mid City Bank." He took her hand, lifted it to his lips, and pressed a kiss to the back of her fingers. Goosebumps raced up her arm. She left her hand in his.

"The bank? Is it safe?" Her voice was a little bit breathless.

"I don't think you'll find much, but we can stop by and ask a teller about a checking account. Just don't get your hopes up." He turned her hand over in his while he was talking, his index finger tracing the lines in her palm.

"I'm kind of excited, is that bad to say?" She wasn't just talking about visiting the bank.

"No, I like your passion and determination to see this through." He continued to play with her fingers, and she shivered slightly. The word passion sent her mind off on a tangent that involved soft sighs and tangled sheets.

"Thank you." Leia looked into Eric's eyes, thanking him for so much more than the promised trip to the bank.

"No more serious talk, bring on those burgers." He released her hand, making room for the waitress to set down their plates.

Leia dug in to the massive plate of food. She and Eric talked about everything and nothing, like the conversations they had shared during the car trip south. Even the most serious topics somehow still resulted in laughter. The burgers were sinfully good.

Sitting at the bar had advantages. One, stellar service, and two, proximity to Eric. His arm was draped behind her back, his finger occasionally caressing her arm. Every time he did it, she swore her temperature rose a few degrees. Her awareness of him was at a new high. The loud restaurant encouraged them to lean close, to touch, and she did. Her left hand rested high on his muscled thigh, and she bent forward to bring her lips near his ear so he could hear her better. Her breast pressed into his arm, and she felt her nipples harden against the lace of her camisole.

Eric switched to water and would occasionally stiffen away from her, glancing around the area looking concerned. She knew he was still worried about her safety, and she was thankful for his vigilance. His care made her feel precious.

With the bill paid, in cash of course, and the last pint glass cleared, Leia didn't want the night to end. Tonight was the best date she'd been on in years. They had laughed and talked and made plans to try each other's favorite Chinese take-out place back in New York to see whose was best. She couldn't wait for him to try Fong's general Tso's chicken.

Eric went to retrieve their coats from the host, who chatted with him briefly. When he returned to the bar, he helped her into her jacket. His hands smoothed the material over her shoulders and down her arms.

"The host arranged a table for us at a nightclub down the block if we want a nightcap. He told me it's a small club that would be quiet even on a night like this. It should be safe enough if you're interested?"

"That sounds great." She was happy to slip her hand in his and be guided from the restaurant.

Eric propelled Leia down a quiet alley and led her to a

restored building that looked like a cross between a Middle Eastern temple and a wedding cake made of marble and brick. The darkened front windows had pointed arches topped with ornate carvings. Through the glass she could make out burgundy velvet banquets and low couches around rose gold tables. The front door swung open, and the seductive voice of a jazz singer flowed out of the candlelit space to meet them.

"Please come in." The elegant man dressed in all black motioned them in the door.

"The host from the gastropub said you'd take care of us," Eric said, slipping him some cash.

The man smiled like the Cheshire cat when he pocketed the bills. He seated them at a loveseat in the far back of the bar, near the stage where a jazz trio fronted by a young woman in a slinky green dress played. Leia sunk into the plush couch, curling into Eric's side. Walking in the cool March air had helped clear her head, but the pleasant glow from a few beers and good food remained.

Eric wrapped an arm around Leia, settling her against his firm chest. The black cashmere sweater he wore over his dark jeans was soft under her cheek. She was content, relaxed in his arms. She should have been worried about her boss, the FBI, and a million other things, but she just wanted to feel this instead. An escape was what she needed. And Eric's arms promised that and so much more.

A twenty-something-year-old waiter with a sleeve of tattoos and a large gauge in his ear appeared with a silver wine bucket; he showed Eric the label on the bottle of blush champagne before popping the cork. The waiter presented them each a flute when he finished pouring.

Eric lifted his glass. "A toast, to a lovely woman, and a perfect evening together." He held her gaze, his eyes dark and smoldering.

"Cheers." Leia clinked her glass with his before taking a sip of the delicious pink sparkling wine. The bubbles tingled on her tongue. She cradled the wine glass in her hand, laying back against Eric's solid chest.

They relaxed, enjoying the talented musicians, the rest of the bar fading into the background. A tray of French macarons magically appeared on their table, and Eric fed a lavender one to her. His fingertips lingered against her lips after she accepted the treat.

"I love this song," she whispered before she began to softly sing along to the classic, *Georgia on My Mind*, her eyes slipping closed. Her voice pitched low, so only he could hear.

Eric's lips slid over hers in a sweet kiss, achingly slow, releasing her mouth just as the last notes of the song wavered in the air.

"You know, I was disappointed this year when I learned you weren't doing my taxes," he said.

Leia looked up at him, a skeptical eyebrow raised. "Really?"

"It's not every day I meet a woman like you," he murmured before bringing their lips together for another kiss.

ELEVEN

ERIC PUSHED her back against the blue front door of the carriage house, kissing her lips and neck while he fumbled with the digital lock. For Leia, the walk back to the rental was a blur of dark streets and stolen embraces, every quiet alleyway a chance for them to explore each other. Their hands entwined, even now, as Eric pinned her against the door.

Finally, a beep announced the door was unlocked. Eric pulled the door open and walked them inside. He shed his sweater and shirt, toeing off his shoes. Leia watched his abs ripple, lit by the nightlights that glowed softly in the entry and stairway.

He stalked toward her, reaching for her. Cool air caressed her stomach as he lifted her sweater off, revealing the camisole she wore underneath. He growled when his hands dove under the lace. Her spine arched, thrusting her breasts into his palms and pushing the camisole's bra up.

Eric pressed her back, helping her sit on the second step of the narrow wooden staircase. He sunk to his knees before her, tugging her boots from her feet and then dragging her leggings off her splayed legs.

"Leia." He breathed her name over the soft skin of her hip as he trailed his lips along her skin. He slipped one finger under the wet satin that hid her core. She sucked in a sharp breath as he teased her folds, promising more.

She braced her knees on the narrow walls, her head tilting back, her moan echoing in the stairway. Reaching forward, she tangled a hand in Eric's dark silky hair, boldly urging his mouth toward her aching center. She anticipated his first taste of her as he tugged aside her panties and slicked his tongue over her.

He was voracious. Her sole focus became his mouth feasting on her delicate flesh. Desire knotted her belly, growing stronger with every sweep of his tongue. He grazed his teeth over her clit dragging her closer to the edge.

"Eric, yes, please." She gasped and ground her hips into his skillful mouth. She wanted her release. She wanted him inside her. Spread, reckless, and willing on the hard stairs, she begged to come. Eric had tapped a spring of need in her that no man had ever released.

He gave her what she needed, his finger parting her, sliding deep inside. Again, Leia begged, gasping his name. His finger shifted, finding a spot that pushed her over the edge. Her legs quivered, her breath stopped, and she crashed over, his name on her lips.

Eric leaned over her, his fingers still buried in her wetness, and found her mouth. He kissed her as the last waves of her orgasm rippled through her. As the fog of her release cleared, she still burned with desire. She wanted more.

Her breath was returning to normal. He pulled back, kneeling between her legs, treating her to a view of his erection straining against his fly. Enthralled, she watched as he stroked himself through the denim while drinking in the sight of her on the stairs.

WANTON WAS the best word Eric could think of to describe the sight before him. Leia's eyes were half-closed, her lacy bra top shoved up over her pert breasts, and her black panties twisted to expose her pussy as she lay draped over the bottom steps. Her musky sweetness filled the cramped stairway, and his cock ached to thrust into her. He needed to be inside her.

"Bedroom, upstairs," he said.

Pulling Leia up, he turned her around and started her stumbling up the stairs. He groaned at the view, a thin black string running between her cheeks. Eric had planned a smooth seduction, never anticipating the desperate need to possess her that was rippling through his body.

When she reached the tiny landing, she paused to tug her lacey camisole off. Eric couldn't stop himself from pressing against her back. Her ass cradled his erection, his body caging her to the wall. He rubbed against her, and she tilted her head back, giving him access to her neck. He gripped her hip, fingers digging into her sweet flesh.

"Leia, I need you," he whispered, nibbling her throat.

"Please," she gasped before pushing back into him, causing Eric to groan in desperation, his cock straining against his zipper.

He tangled his hand in her hair and ground his throbbing erection against her firm ass. His free hand plumped her breast and pinched her nipple into a hard peak. His mouth watered thinking about tasting the hard bud. Reluctantly he stepped back and together they clambered up the last few treacherous steps into the bedroom.

Turning her to face him, he kissed her, one hand still fisted in her hair as he walked them toward the king-sized bed. He was drowning in Leia—her smell, her taste.

Her hands moved from his waist to tug open his pants and push down his underwear. Once his cock was free, she reached for his shaft. Eric watched as her small fingers encircled the head, then slipped down the thick shaft. It was a powerfully erotic image that would be stamped in his memory forever. Her simple touch forced a rasping moan from his throat. He clenched his jaw, willing himself not to come in her hand like a teenager.

He shackled her wrists with his hands. "Later, you can touch."

He pushed her back on to the bed. Shucking his pants and underwear, he followed her down. He stopped to retrieve a condom from his wallet. His fingers were desperate as he pulled her black panties off before he again knelt between her legs. He allowed himself another taste of her slick folds. She gasped and lifted her hips to his mouth. She was so eager and responsive. He dragged his mouth away, searching out the dip of her navel, her skin like molten silk beneath him.

He savored each moan and gasp as he worshiped her breasts, her small nipples hardening under his assault. Every taste of her skin surpassed his fantasies. Using his teeth to nip the tender underside of her breast, he marked her skin. She was his.

Leia's hips were moving under him, a silent plea for him to fill her. Her eyes were closed, and her head tossed back and forth on the pillow. She was desperate, and Eric wanted to give her everything she desired.

He hovered over her, waiting for her eyes to open. He

wanted to see the moment he filled her reflected in her eyes. She stilled and met his gaze. He tore the foil package open.

"Please, Eric."

Fisting his hard cock, he slipped on the condom and teased her opening with the head of his shaft, readying her. He dragged his shaft through the gathered wetness, nudging her clit before moving lower again. The slow slide into Leia's pussy nearly shredded his control. He needed to move, thrust, claim the woman below him.

Leia took every inch of him, her eyes growing heavy, languid as he worked his cock into her tight sheath. Eric watched her accepting him, welcoming him in. Her face was flushed and her swollen lips parted on a sigh. Their gazes met and she whimpered his name.

He braced his weight on his arms taking a moment to enjoy being buried deep inside her. Leia wrapped her lithe legs around him and arched up, begging him to move. Her walls clamped down, squeezing him tight, bliss raced up his spine.

It was her first shudder combined with her nails biting into his shoulders that pushed him into motion. His control disappeared; he had to move. He pumped into her, searching for the rhythm that would satisfy them both. Finesse was lost in the struggle for release. Entwined on the crisp white sheets, they clung to each other. Deep thrusts and messy kisses, mouths crashing together between ragged breaths.

He pinned her to the bed, holding down her wrists, regaining some control. She was his now, his fantasy come to life. The brutal frenzy slowed to measured thrusts in and out of her, again and again. At his mercy, she begged him to let her come. She twisted below him, her face flushed and eyes wide, his name spilling from her mouth with each gasp.

When she let go, she came apart, trembling. Her legs wrapped tight around him, and her back bowed. She shouted her release into his chest, her teeth sinking into his pec as she spiraled apart. He cradled her against his body for a breath.

"Leia, open your eyes, come back to me."

Her lids fluttered open, and her gaze locked with his. He pushed deep into her; she shuddered in pleasure as he thrust faster and harder. His need grew and his control slipped. He drove his hips into her. She was coming again, a silent scream, she rippled around him, their eyes still locked. A shudder ripped through him. He threw his head back and shouted as a wave of pleasure crashed over him. His cock jerked emptying inside her.

He slowly floated back to earth, dragging Leia against his chest as he collapsed to the side. Their harsh breathing slowed. He pressed a kiss to her head, his eyes closed. She mumbled his name against his skin. A smile curved his lips —satisfied was an understatement. He was spent, and the soft snore from Leia led him to believe she was as well. He reluctantly rolled away to deal with the condom before he could fall asleep with her.

LEIA STRETCHED. Waking up in Eric's arms was a lovely way to start a Sunday. In the last week, her entire world had been flipped upside down. But this felt right. His arms sheltered her from the upheaval all around her. She wasn't sure if she was looking for stability in a time of crisis, but last night had been fantastic. Was this attraction between them the result of proximity and danger? Would it fade once the FBI finally stepped in to do their job?

The part of last night where they had clothes on had felt like a date; Eric even called it that. And compared to her most recent dates, it had been a great one. And after, it was incendiary. He was an incredible lover. Was *lover* the right term? Or fling. *He's not a one-night stand, but would he want to be my boyfriend? Would I want him as my boyfriend?* She cringed at the term *boyfriend*—the word *boy* would never apply to Eric.

She sighed, shifting her naked back against his chest. She had no regrets, but she also wasn't sure how this changed their situation. Or how this survived once the FBI stepped in to protect her. Maybe they were just two people who crossed each other's paths at the wrong time, their lives never quite lining up the right way to have anything more than a brief moment together. If this was all she got, she wanted to enjoy the moment.

Eric's arm wrapped tightly around her waist; he nuzzled his morning scruff against her neck. "Morning, beautiful. Should we find some coffee? Or can I convince you to stay right here?"

His hand slipped up to cradle her breast, and his hard cock pressed against the curve of her ass.

She decided there was something better than waking up to a cup of coffee.

TWELVE

THE RED BRICK bank building was on Broughton Street wedged between a funky diner and an art supply store. The street was an eclectic mix of businesses that catered to college students and others that were angling for tourist dollars.

Dressed in a new SCAD sweatshirt and her skinny jeans, Leia walked into the only branch of Savannah Mid City Bank. The lobby had two tellers and a security guard but was otherwise deserted. Most of Savannah was taking Monday off to recover from the weekend St Patrick's Day festival and rest up for tomorrow's parade.

The first teller, a sleepy-looking college-aged girl with black hair and a nose piercing, waved Leia over to the counter. The movement pulled up her sleeve to display a colorful tattoo under her conservative button-down shirt.

"May I help you?" she drawled, her heavy southern accent a jarring contrast to her goth art student looks.

"Can I have some information on opening a checking account?" Leia asked as she looked around the bank; it was pretty typical.

"Yes, ma'am, I will be right back." The goth girl wandered off to a back office, leaving Leia to wait.

When she returned, the teller passed Leia a stack of pamphlets and launched into a very professional comparison between the various accounts offered. Leia nodded and agreed when it seemed appropriate, listening with half an ear while looking around the bank lobby, memorizing every detail. She noted that there was a row of private offices along the back and security cameras in the corners.

When the girl stopped talking, Leia blinked. That was it; her reason for coming to the city was a bust. All she had to show for the trip was a handful of brochures. Discouraged, she forced a smiled for the teller before thanking her and collecting the papers. She dragged her feet as she wandered to the parking lot to find Eric leaning against the Jag.

"So?" he asked.

"It's a bank. A plain old fashioned small-ish bank. Nothing exciting." Her shoulders slumped, and she waited for Eric's I told you so… which never came. She was glad he refrained from saying it was a waste of time, since she was already telling herself that.

"Come on, let's head back to the carriage house, eat lunch, or something." Eric opened her car door, helping her into the seat. He rubbed her arm, encouraging her to shake it off.

During the short drive across town, Leia was quiet. She didn't know if she wanted to scream or cry. The trip to the bank hadn't gotten her any new information to help untangle Sal's files for the FBI.

She bolted for the front door of the rental as soon as Eric stopped the car. Once inside, she tossed the pamphlets from the bank on the coffee table and thumped down on the overstuffed couch.

By the time Eric walked in, she was fighting back tears. Eric sat down next to her and pulled her into his lap.

"Talk," he ordered.

"It's not fair." Leia crossed her arms over her chest, pissed at her circumstances. "I'm doing the right thing. I went to the FBI. It's Monday. Did they call that answering service number you gave Simms?"

"No, I would've told you."

"I wanted that bank to be the key. I hate it when I do this. I get an idea in my head, and I go for it. I just trudge forward forgetting the consequences. My bad planning is why Sal is after me. My schemes always fail. I just keep screwing things up." She buried her head in his chest, tears leaking onto his shirt.

"We'll figure this out."

"Why? Why do you even want to be here, putting your life on hold for me?" Leia hated the idea that Eric was trapped babysitting her.

"Look at me. You are the best person I know. You're doing the right thing. It's going to take time. I want to help you succeed, and I'm not complaining about spending time with you." Eric met her gaze, drying a few tears from her face before giving her a sweet soft kiss.

Leia clung to him, his words giving her hope that this mess might somehow work out. Hope that she could have a normal life again. She sighed and relaxed into his chest.

"I'm sorry I'm upset about that stupid bank. You told me I wouldn't find anything." She stayed curled in his lap, listening to his heartbeat. The steady rhythm reminded her of how wonderful it felt to sleep in his arms last night. She feathered a few soft kisses over his neck and under his chin.

"Leia, did you look at any of the paperwork the bank gave you?" Eric asked. He was staring over her head at the pile of pamphlets she'd dumped on the coffee table.

"No, it's just junk about opening a new account."

Leaning forward, almost dumping her off his lap, he snatched a tri-fold brochure out of the mess and held it in front of her. It was titled: *Cyber Investing and Bitcoin at Savannah Mid City Bank.*

Leia flipped it open. The inside was useless information on the dangers of Bitcoin for the novice and a sales pitch for bitcoin investor trainings. On the back was a basic map. It had one star over the main branch's Broughton Street location, and a second star over the town of Pooler, Georgia. The map was labeled: Bitcoin ATM locations.

"What is a Bitcoin ATM? And where is Pooler, Georgia?" she asked.

"Bitcoin ATMs are just like a regular ATMs, but they let you buy and sell Bitcoin for cash. A few of my more paranoid customers like to pay me in Bitcoin," Eric told her with an explanatory shrug. "Pooler, Georgia, looks like it's out by I-95. It might be a nice place to drive to on a Monday afternoon. Want to go?"

Leia raised a skeptical eyebrow. "Think it will be worth the drive?"

"I think it's curious and has more potential than the bank lobby you visited today. Everything about Bitcoin makes my skin crawl."

POOLER WAS ABOUT thirty minutes outside Savannah off I-95; the only reason Leia could see that anyone would stop there was the RV dealership. It had acres of new Winnebagos lined up along the highway to entice shoppers. Otherwise, the town was a few old strip malls, an auto repair place, and a couple run-down churches.

When they exited the highway, Eric pointed the Jag

toward the other main attraction in Pooler: a new mega gas station that had everything from frozen yogurt machines and gourmet coffee to a beer cave.

A steady stream of cars pulling in off Interstate 95 stopped at the station for a quick pitstop, but Leia could pick out a few customers that looked more like locals. Eric slid the Jag into a parking place on the near side of the convenience store, backing into the spot.

"Check out across the street," he said, gesturing to a dilapidated off-brand gas station. Its marquee sign by the road had inflated fuel prices posted with missing lettering. The station's pumps looked ready to rust into the ground, and two had bags over the handles, indicating they were out of service.

"Wow, how is that place staying open?"

"Might be its bitcoin ATM."

"Seriously! That's the address on the pamphlet?" Leia rechecked the address on the brochure against the faded numbers she could barely decipher on the station's front.

"Yep."

"What now?"

"We watch." Eric got out of the car, walking around to the trunk. Leia watched him in the side mirror as he retrieved a black tactical backpack before getting back in.

From the bag, he fished out a pair of digital binoculars, a note pad, and a pen. He passed her the paper and pen while holding the binoculars ready in his lap. He didn't have to wait long. A lowrider Chevy Impala with blinged-out chrome wheels, extra dark window tint, and whitewall tires coasted into the parking lot. Eric had her write down the make of the car and the license plate as he read it off through the binoculars.

The car came to a stop right in front of the gas

station's small convenience store, and a young guy wearing low slung baggy jeans and a black skull cap hustled inside. Next to her, Eric cursed the glare on the front windows of the gas station; he couldn't see what was going on inside. About three minutes later, the dude came swaggering back out to the lowrider, got in the passenger side, and the driver peeled out of the crappy gas station, barreling toward the I-95 on-ramp.

"So he went in and bought smokes?" Leia asked.

"Don't know, can't see." Eric leaned back in his seat, arms crossed, waiting to see what else might happen. His long fingers drummed a staccato rhythm on the steering wheel.

Leia sighed; she felt like this was a wild goose chase, just like the bank location in town. But she would keep her mouth shut for now. Maybe she could get them some frozen yogurt while Eric had his stakeout.

Eric put the car in drive and moved it to the other side of the mega gas station's parking area. The new line of sight improved the glare on the front window, and with the binoculars, he'd be able to see inside the crappy gas station.

She reached her hand out for a turn with the binoculars. The inside of the station was even more derelict than the outside, with dingy beer posters on the wall, dirty linoleum floors, and empty shelves.

"Do you see it?" Eric asked.

"Yep." On the back wall, she could see about half of the Bitcoin logo on what looked like a standard ATM. Resting the binoculars on the armrest, she leaned back in her seat, eyes closed for a while.

Eric's elbow jabbed her side, getting her attention. He had the binoculars to his face and was reading off another car make and plate number. This time it was a souped-up red mud truck. The guy driving had to leap out of the cab, the tires were so big, before he walked in the station.

"What's he doing?" she asked.

"He knows whoever is behind the counter, just gave one of them a fist bump. He's at the ATM now; I can't see much but his left arm. I think he's pulling something out of his back pocket, cash maybe. Hard to tell from here. That's it. He's coming out."

The guy emerged from the store; he readjusted his faded trucker hat before climbing up into his massive truck and turning back toward I-95.

The next hour was more of the same. A seedy car or truck would pull into the gas station across the way; a person would go inside and use the bitcoin ATM and leave. Most seemed to know the people working behind the counter, and they all got back on the highway after their transaction. Eric was quiet, except for giving her the vehicle information to write down, but waves of tension flowed from him.

"Eric, what are we watching?" Leia's question broke the strained silence in the car.

"WHAT DO you know about crime on the east coast of the United States?" Eric asked Leia, the tight feeling in his stomach getting worse every time a new vehicle pulled into the lot across the way. Leia was in deep; this was more than just cleaning a little dirty money. He hated that he was right; Sal's clients had to be working together.

"I don't know, not much," she answered.

"For years, Interstate 95 has been a pipeline to move the illegal drugs that South American cartels smuggle into Florida to bigger cities like New York. Drugs move north, and money comes south. The network ships everything from pot to heroin over I-95; every off-ramp is a way to distribute product to dealers.

"The rural south is a source for firearms bought at illegal or underregulated gun shows with dirty money. The guns flow into urban areas with stricter firearm laws. Guns have been part of the supply chain for decades. And knowing Pavel Oblonsky is on Sal's client list, I think it's safe to say the pipeline has expanded to include women too.

"I think what we're seeing is a drop-off point for cash from deals done all along the I-95 corridor. Pooler is an excellent location. It's outside of Florida where law enforcement is better, south of the congestion of DC, and Atlanta is only a few hours west."

He needed more information. The leap in logic he was making was giant, way too big of a jump for the FBI to make. Protecting Leia was his only concern, but part of that was getting the FBI to arrest Sal's clients. If he had to spoon-feed the FBI the information on this network, he would do it.

Leia had threaded her fingers through his while he spoke, hanging on to his hand.

Intel was key. "I need to get inside, see what I can find out," he said. "I'm going to walk over. You pull around that side road and park behind the station." He was regretting the flashy Jaguar, but there was nothing he could do about the car now.

Leia's eyes were wide. Before she could try to talk him out of it, he grabbed a ball cap from his gear bag, his sunglasses, and got out of the car. He dumped the gear bag back in the trunk as he passed.

Trying to look more like the unsavory characters that had been frequenting the station, Eric half untucked his shirt, unbuttoning it to show the undershirt he had on while he waited to cross the road. From the corner of his eye, he watched Leia move the Jag behind the station.

She had the car in the perfect spot if he needed a quick exit. *Good girl.*

THIRTEEN

ERIC PULLED open the grimy gas station door. The peeling letters stuck to the glass proclaimed the station to be the *Confederate Gas n Go*. The nauseating smell of old hot dogs cooking on rollers wafted out to meet him before he crossed the threshold. The overhead lights buzzed, and an ancient coffee pot sat empty on a counter next to a full beer cooler. The store had sparsely stocked shelves, other than an impressive display of vape pens, and a turnstile rack of personalized Georgia license plate keychains near the door.

Now that he was inside, not just looking in the window, he could see the two guys behind the counter. One wore a stained work shirt with the name Ray-Ray on the front. The redneck looked about forty and had a wad of chewing tobacco poking out his bottom lip. His greasy hair hung long in the back, and when he looked up at Eric, he didn't smile. The other employee sat leaning back on a three-legged stool; he was younger, fitter, and meaner looking than Ray-Ray. Eric would guess he was the muscle hired to guard the ATM.

Eric walked to the ATM and pushed a few buttons; there was no way he would log into his account from here. That would be like asking Sal Marino to come to Georgia and kill him personally.

Behind him, the store's front door clanged open. Eric glanced over his shoulder to see a short skinny white guy walk in. The twenty-something wore a wife-beater shirt and baggy ripped jeans. He knew Ray-Ray. The kid looked more like a wannabe New York City thug than rural Georgia local. He was all swagger; Eric knew the type. Reminded him of peacocks, tough until you leaned on them.

"My man! Ray-Ray! Busy day in here," the guy said, pointing at Eric. "No point in waiting. You got the key to the shitter?"

Ray-Ray tossed the guy a naked barbie doll; Eric assumed the restroom key was attached to it.

In an instant, Eric knew he had a golden opportunity to get more intel. He counted to ten, then turned and walked out the door of the *Confederate Gas n Go* after the wife-beater shirt guy. Ray-Ray and the muscle never looked up.

The bathroom was on the backside of the convenience store, and Leia had the Jag parked about eight steps away. Adrenaline rushed through his veins; it'd been a while since he'd kidnaped anyone.

The barbie doll was hanging from the bathroom key that was in the outside door lock. Eric swung the door open. The bathroom was as small and disgusting as Eric had imagined.

"Fuck, man, I'm in here!" the guy yelled. He was sitting on the toilet, pants around his ankles, looking really pissed off.

Eric threw a hard punch that connected with the

dude's jaw, knocking him off the toilet and out cold. The guy was splayed out on the nasty bathroom floor, not moving. Eric savored the sting in his knuckles, shaking out his right hand; it felt good to be doing something to help Leia besides sitting at the computer or hiding.

Jogging back to the Jag, he knocked on the driver side window. "Pop the trunk," he yelled through the glass to Leia. He saw the question on her face. She knew he was up to something.

Riffling through his gear bag in the trunk, he found a roll of duct tape that would work to secure his new friend for a trip to the Georgia woods. Tape in hand, he headed back to the bathroom.

"LEIA, DRIVE NOW," Eric said when he got in the car.

"What the hell just happened? Is there an unconscious guy with no pants in our trunk?" Leia got the Jag in gear and was heading toward I-95. She couldn't believe that Eric tossed a half-naked guy in the trunk. This felt a lot like breaking the law. Freaked out, she focused on driving the car and not what might happen next.

"Not the highway."

In Eric's hand was a phone she'd never seen before, and after he turned it off, he put it in the glovebox. He directed her through the center of Pooler, past the edge of civilization, until they reached a wildlife area. After winding down a small dirt path for a couple of miles, he pointed at a small clearing in the trees and had her pull over. She guided the Jag with a white-knuckle grip, breathing in quick ragged gasps like she'd just run a sprint. Eric appeared calm.

"Leia, it's going to be fine," he said, his hand covering

hers on the wheel. She looked down to see the split skin over three of his knuckles oozing blood. It didn't feel like it was going to be fine.

He half turned in his seat to face her. "The guy in the trunk knows what's going on at that gas station. He's going to fill in a few blanks for us."

"Okay," she sputtered, her hands still locked in a death grip on the wheel. Eric's calm was inconceivable to her.

"I'm going to have to encourage him to talk. You need to let me do what I need to do. Is that clear?"

"What are you going to do?" Her anxiety ratcheted up another notch.

"You don't need to watch if you can't handle it, just turn your back. What I do need is your ears. I need you to write down everything, names, dates, places. Any information he gives us that might be important later."

"I can't be part of this." she faced Eric, shaking her head no, her hands trembling. This wasn't something she could do; it wasn't something she wanted to see Eric do.

He framed her face with his hands. "You already are part of this. We need information. I'm just going to rough him up a bit. I need you to take notes and not get in the way. You can cry it out as soon as we're done, okay?"

She nodded, her tears threatening to spill. She would rather cry it out now and let their hostage go free.

He leaned in close and rested his forehead on hers, their breath mingling. She wrapped her hands around his wrists, the connection helping her regain control. His pulse beat evenly under her fingers.

"If we had more time, more resources, we could try another way, but we don't. He is the best lead we have. I have to do something to keep you safe." He pressed his lips to hers in an achingly soft kiss that hinted at the fierce emotions he was keeping in check.

They pulled apart, and Leia looked out the front windshield of the Jag. The shade of the towering Southern pines cast deep shadows, making the afternoon feel like dusk. It was a peaceful scene that stretched out in front of her, a fallen log and small grassy meadow with the first shoots of spring grass. She reached for the discarded pad and pen in the center console, wrapping her unwilling hands around them. Today was like the day in Sal's office when she stole the data files. Today, she needed to do this for families victimized by her boss and his clients.

Her eyes refocused on Eric. "Okay, I'm ready."

Her hands were steady when she reached for the door handle.

LARRY—THEY decided his name was Larry because that's what the tattoo on his left knuckles read—was finally conscious. He was duct-taped to a large pine tree wearing his white wife-beater shirt and a faded pair of smiley face boxer shorts. Eric had Larry's right hand stretched out on a fallen log and was explaining that if he failed to provide the information needed, he would lose a few fingers today.

Leia pushed her nausea down for the third or fourth time, hoping that Larry would cooperate and she would never know if Eric was bluffing or not. She was sure she would never look at Eric the same if she watched him sever a man's finger.

Leia guessed that Larry might be five and a half feet tall. It was hard to judge height when he was being hauled around by Eric like a sack of garbage. She was pretty sure she was taller than him. He had floppy blond hair, one gold tooth, and an ugly collection of poorly chosen tattoos scattered over his skinny frame. The purple bruise Eric gifted him with on his jaw wasn't helping his looks any either.

A string of inventive curses rained down on Eric. Larry had a colorful vocabulary and foul mouth. He punctuated his rant by spitting at Eric. Rage radiated off Eric, and he slowly raised his arm, backhanding Larry across the face. More than the physical pain, it was the combination of Eric's expression and his slow controlled movements that seem to register with Larry. He shut up and closed his eyes, leaning his head back on the tree, like he just realized how screwed he was.

The sympathy Leia had for Larry before meeting the man was rapidly dissipating. In the few minutes he'd been conscious, he called Leia a whore, threatened Eric with castration, and confirmed that he worked for Pavel Oblonsky because he liked the pussy.

"Let's start with the basics, shall we, Larry? What do you do for Oblonsky?" Eric asked.

Larry kept his mouth shut, biting his split lip. Leia could tell that the weaselly little man was weighing the repercussions—Eric's fist right here versus Oblonsky's punishment in the future. Apparently, he was more concerned about his boss.

From his pants pocket Eric retrieved a black folding combat knife. This was what she didn't want to see. Standing a few steps back from Larry's outstretched legs, Eric slowly opened the knife and leisurely engaged the blade lock, making sure Larry watched each step in the process. From Leia's perspective across the small clearing, the five-inch blade and spear point looked deadly.

When Eric stepped toward Larry, Leia turned her head. She wouldn't interfere, but she couldn't watch, either. She focused on the notepad in her hands, scribbling in the corner of the blank page, keeping her eyes focused on the black marks she was making while willing herself to keep it together.

"Larry, I'll start here on your pinky finger. Don't imagine you need that," Eric said, his voice calm.

Larry started to snivel, his incessant whimpering drowning out the birdsong and other noises of the woods. She stayed focused on the pen, drawing random patterns on the page.

Larry's scream ripped through the air, startling her. She reminded herself not to look over at the men and scrambled to retrieve the pen that had fallen from her grasp. *Eric said he wasn't a criminal.* She was sure torture was a crime.

"You made me do that, Larry. I need details. Start talking about Oblonsky and that gas station. It can only get worse for you." Eric's ice-cold voice cut through Larry's blubbering.

"I'm a driver. I just drive an eighteen-wheeler. I don't even know what's in it most of the time." Sputtering through hysterical tears, he seemed younger with his swagger drained away. Larry spilled a flood of information with no additional prompting from Eric.

"The ATM is where I drop off Oblonsky's cash I get when I deliver a load for him. I take the money to the Gas N Go, feed it in that Bitcoin machine, and go on my next job. The other guys that come in there are like me, low-level dealers, gun runners, drivers, whatever. We aren't a team or nothing. Rumor is that some fancy-ass New York accountant cleans all that dirty Bitcoin money and gives it back to our bosses. Bet that dude is making bank. Ya know?"

Leia wondered at how helpful Larry had become. It seemed the pain from his severed finger wasn't slowing down his mouth at all.

"Who's Ray-Ray and the other guy behind the counter?" Eric asked, ignoring Larry's question.

"Ray-Ray is just a businessman. That new gas station was going to put him underwater. He got the ATM before the new station even had a building permit. The scary dude behind the counter is Ray-Ray's cousin, just got outta jail, works there 'cause he's on parole."

"Names?"

Larry rattled off the names of a few other guys that used the ATM, the guys behind the counter at the gas station, and even the name of the parole officer for Ray-Ray's cousin. Leia wrote down every detail. Her hand was steady as she filled the page with Larry's inside information.

"How do you get paid?" Eric was leaning against a nearby tree with the same hard stare he'd fixed in place since pulling Larry out of the trunk.

A bit of Larry's swagger was reappearing; apparently, the loss of a finger wasn't enough to humble this kid.

"Fuck, man, I get a check, a legitimate one, you know like with a W2 and all that official shit. I'm on payroll for a real company that Mr. Oblonsky owns." He said the word "legitimate" with about six syllables. He continued talking, and Leia added to her notes—the name of his employer and the employers of a few other ATM users.

"Yeah, not a big fan of your boss, Mr. Oblonsky. What else can you tell me about him?"

Larry didn't utter a sound. The chatty fountain of information was drying up, but the fear of retribution from Oblonsky was still there.

"Larry, we aren't done. You don't get to decide when to stop talking."

Larry whimpered again. Leia shot a glance in his direction; Eric was still leaning against the tree. Larry looked nervous, chewing that already abused lip.

"Why don't you tell me why you're in town?"

"St Patrick's Day."

Leia could hear the smirk in Larry's answer. The crunch of Eric's hand against Larry's face came just moments later.

Larry was wailing again. "You broke my fucking nose!"

"It could be worse." Eric knelt next to Larry's vulnerable hand again, and Leia spun away when she saw the glint of the knife Eric brandished.

"No, no. Shit, okay, Mr. Oblonsky has a big shipment coming in at the port in Brunswick tomorrow night. I'm the driver. There's a new client in Jacksonville, some big player. Mr. Oblonsky is meeting me at the shipyard tomorrow night for the unloading and going to follow me down to Florida."

"Ship name? Container number? What else do you have for me, Larry?"

"The Narcissus." Larry deflated, wrung out, the betrayal to his boss complete. His chin tucked into his chest, and he'd caved.

Leia underlined the ship's name in her notes.

"Thank you, Larry." Eric patted him on the shoulder.

"You got all that?" Eric asked, looking at Leia.

She nodded and walked back to the car, settling into the passenger seat. She hoped the list of names on the notepad was enough to motivate the FBI.

Eric walked around the clearing with Larry's pants dragging behind him. Confused by his random path, Leia kept watching. Finally, Eric tossed the pants up into a tree, high enough that the vertically challenged Larry was going to have some problems retrieving them.

Eric walked toward Larry, the knife open in his hand. When Eric leaned over him, Leia's breath caught in her throat. She fumbled for the door latch. Eric couldn't kill him. It wasn't worth it. Before she could bolt from the car, Eric stood back up. Larry struggled frantically against the tape holding him to the tree, yelling muffled curses at Eric's retreating back. Leia let out her breath, sagging into the seat.

"That went well," Eric said as he turned the car back toward the main road. He was smiling like he just got back from a nature walk.

That kid was missing a finger, maybe two. He wasn't a great guy, but couldn't he bleed to death or die of some kind of infection? *Is it bad form to render aid after being an accessory to torture?*

"Yes, best maiming ever," she snapped. She couldn't handle this.

"I didn't maim the stupid kid." Eric's voice sounded like he was disappointed by her accusation.

"I heard the screams."

"What you heard was a dumb kid getting scared enough to think I would cut off his finger. I've cut myself worse chopping lettuce."

"You swear you didn't permanently damage him?" Leia stared at his profile as he drove, looking for any sign he might lie to her.

"A bandaid and some antibiotic ointment, he'll be as good as new in a couple days." He turned away from the road to look at Leia's doubtful face. "You believe me, right?"

She paused. She believed him, but she also realized he would have gone farther to get what he needed. She couldn't decide if the uneasiness she felt was because Eric could do what he did and more, or the fact that he was doing it for her.

"I believe you, but how far would you have gone?" she asked.

"I told you before; I don't do hypotheticals. I sized up the kid and knew he was all talk. Yes, I could have been wrong, but I wasn't. I don't want you to over-analyze this. I only hurt him enough to scare him. It was a fair trade for that information." Eric's hand found Leia's where it rested in her lap. He threaded their fingers together and brought the back of her hand to his lips for a kiss.

"Think he'll make it back to his car alright?" Leia couldn't stop herself from asking the question.

Eric huffed a laugh under his breath before he answered. "Unfortunately, for society, guys like Larry are human cockroaches. Harder to kill than you think." He was still holding her hand.

She squeezed his hand and studied his profiles as he drove. He'd done so much for her it was beyond what she could ever have hoped. He was on her side one hundred percent. She started this because it was the right thing to do. She'd been alone and everything had to be a secret. Now she had a coconspirator, a teammate. It was a huge relief to share the weight with someone.

FOURTEEN

"SEND ME YOUR ACCOUNTING REPORT." Eric glanced over at Leia. She was mostly asleep curled up under an afghan on the couch in the carriage house.

She stretched like an oversized cat, her back arching, thrusting her small breasts against her thin tee shirt. She yawned and tangled one of her hands in her hair, trying to smooth the disarray.

"Okay. What time is it?"

Eric checked the clock on his computer screen. One a.m. Tuesday. At least he was almost done.

"Late."

In the last few hours, he'd combined the list of names from Larry with the other breadcrumbs he'd been assembling on the crime syndicate. The report he created from cross-referencing all the data with what he'd found on the dark web was a comprehensive analysis of a criminal enterprise of staggering size.

If spoon-feeding the FBI a case was the only way he could get them to help protect Leia, so be it. Oblonsky was in Savannah, and it was eating away at his confidence that he could continue to hide and successfully defend her by himself.

Before the last few days with Leia, Eric thought being alone was for the best. No partner to betray him, no woman to curb his independence. A week ago, he would never have thought for a second that his existence was lonely or made him vulnerable. Leia's situation had forced him to think about more than just his safety. The risk of betrayal paled in comparison to the fear that he couldn't protect her alone.

Leia was opening his eyes, making him reevaluate the cold gray life he'd been living since killing Max. Her presence challenged his habits. He kept his life simple by only dealing with cold hard facts and not allowing emotions to color his decisions.

A bing from his laptop indicated the email from Leia with her report had arrived. He added it to the secure cloud folder that he would be sharing with Agent Simms in a few moments.

"Thank you," he said.

Eric typed Simms's email address into the *To* line of the completed email. All he needed to do was click send, and the FBI would have everything they could need to justify giving Leia protection.

"This is it, Leia. We're sending them everything. You ready?"

She gave an earnest nod.

He clicked send and pushed his chair back from the bistro table. Resting his elbows on his knees, he dropped his head in his hands. He wanted that to be the smartest thing he'd ever done.

STRESS AND LACK of sleep were weighing heavy on Eric. She'd hoped that once the files were sent his anxiety would lessen. They had laid all their accusations out for the FBI to follow. Now they had to wait.

She hated that her presence in his life had done this to him, made him second guess his actions. She'd thrust the responsibility for her safety onto Eric, and he'd become her white knight. Someone against all the odds that she trusted to protect her. But now, he looked strung out, stressed, and worried that their decision to trust the FBI might not be the right one.

Leia rose and went to the kitchen where she poured the last glass of red wine. He lifted his head when she approached.

She pressed the overfilled wine glass into his hands and moved behind him to rub his neck.

"Have a sip. It's good and might help you relax." She worked on loosening a knot in his shoulder. He moaned into the wine glass as she dug her fingers in deeper.

She trailed her fingers up his back and used her thumbs to knead the tendons on the sides of his neck. She could feel his throat work as he took another swallow of the wine. He leaned back into her touch, his eyes closed, his body relaxing under her attention.

Leia cradled Eric's head against her chest, trailing her fingers gently over his face and ghosting a caress over the arch of his eyebrows, down the sharp rise of his cheek-bones. His stubble was rough against the pads of her fingers. As her hands traveled over his face, the lines on his forehead relaxed.

Her hands slid down toward the neck of his soft tee shirt and slipped under the material, seeking the warmth of skin-to-skin contact. She knew that under her right palm was the mark she'd left on his pec the first night they were together.

She drew in a breath; her nose picked up Eric's unique scent, citrusy and woodsy. She dipped her head and kissed his lips. The kiss was fleeting; Eric remained passive beneath her mouth.

She stepped around the chair to stand between his open knees. His eyes opened, and he lifted his head to take another large sip of wine. After he swallowed, she leaned in for another kiss, and Eric allowed her free rein. The taste of the rich wine flooded her mouth.

A pliant Eric was new, and Leia enjoyed the moment. Being responsible for his pleasure increased her desire. Nudging his head back, she licked and sucked his throat while her hands worked to open his pants.

She freed his erection and palmed his already hard length. The heat and weight of him in her hand stirred her need. She wanted him desperate for her touch.

She slid his pants and briefs down, dropping to her knees in front of him. She stroked his length and looked up at his face. His eyes were closed and his head tipped back, resting on the chair. In one hand he still cradled the almost empty wine glass.

She teased the head of his cock with her breath, letting her lips drag over him, then opened and took him inside her mouth. He groaned above her but remained still, allowing her to taste him. She worked slowly, up and down his length, taking him as deeply as she could, over and over.

Leia wanted to push the limits of his control, find out if he would remain passive and accept what she gave him. Her thighs were slick with need. Knowing that she held the undivided attention of the man before her made her want him even more.

She paused, letting him press against the back of her throat. She flicked her glance up to see he was watching her; their eyes met, and a tremor shook his body. He dropped his head back again, and she resumed her deliberate pace, reaching her hand to cup his balls. He exhaled her name. Leia rejoiced, hearing her name slip from his lips.

She pulled back, the length of his shaft scraping gently over her teeth, until she could nibble at the head. Leia heard the wine glass tumble to the floor and roll away; Eric wrapped his hands around the wood spindles below the seat of the chair. His hips lifted, begging for more. Leia plunged back down, accepting as much of his length as she could, pushing her limits.

The first salty drops of his pre-cum filled her mouth; Eric's body bowed up off the chair, his hips flexed toward her mouth, suspended between ecstasy and agony. She teased him, leaving him balanced on the edge of release. He groaned like he was in pain.

She pulled back, resting on her heels. "Do you want more?"

"Yes," he growled.

She rose from her knees, stripping her clothes off. Eric's eyes devoured each inch of skin she revealed. She fished a condom from her open purse on the kitchen counter. Holding it between her teeth, she straddled his legs, dragging her wetness over his thighs. She ripped open a condom packet and then unrolled the latex over his throbbing length.

He reached for her waist, but she shook her head and grasped his wrists, returning them to the rungs of the chair. To punish him for his presumption, she dragged her teeth over the cords of his neck.

He moaned, his head falling back, gifting her with his surrender.

"Please," he begged, his breathing rough and gasping.

She inched forward on his lap, pressing her dripping wet folds against his hard cock, teasing her clit on him. She slid back and forth over the hardness, enjoying the sensation, her hands shoved up Eric's shirt to feel his hot skin, the crinkle of his chest hair.

Under her, Eric was straining, lifting his hips, following the rhythm she set, wordlessly pleading for more. She couldn't ignore her need any longer. Rising on her toes, she positioned herself over him, and took his shaft into her. His length filling her completely, she savored the connection of their bodies.

"Oh God, yes, Leia," he sighed when fully engulfed in her heat.

She rode him hard, her arms twined around his neck for support as he thrust up against her. The angle pushed his cock deep, hitting a spot that made her gasp. When she slid forward, her breasts scraped over the scattered hair on his chest, the added sensation like lightning bolts. They were both straining, chasing their orgasms. Goosebumps rose on her skin. Her body was overwhelmed, overstimulated. Her even rhythm grew disjointed, frantic, as she twisted and rubbed against him.

"So close. Come with me?" she whimpered into his ear.

He groaned in response. "I need to touch you."

"Yes."

Eric's hands, suddenly free from self-imposed restraint, wrapped around her waist, helping her to fuck him. He was impossibly hard and thick. A few good thrusts pushed Leia over her edge. A scream ripped from her throat. She shook as a wave of crippling pleasure washed over her. Moments later, he shuddered and poured himself into her.

Limp and exhausted, she tried to lift herself off Eric's lap, but he pulled her close, nuzzling her neck while dropping stray kisses on her damp skin.

"Thank you, beautiful," he murmured in her ear. "That was spectacular."

A heady combination of pride and lust swirled in Leia's chest at his words. If this was just a fling, she was getting in way too deep. He made her bold and brave in bed, gave her the confidence to enjoy his pleasure and her own. If this relationship had an expiration date, she wasn't going to waste a moment.

FIFTEEN

"COME ON, ERIC, LET'S GO!" Leia was tying the laces of her running shoes, excited to head out and save seats for the St Patrick's Day parade.

Still nursing his coffee, Eric joined her at the front door, dragging on his jacket.

"Leia, it's barely eight in the morning. The parade won't start for hours."

"Yes, but we need a good spot so we can see. I love parades. Thank you for agreeing we could risk going." She stood and kissed him on the cheek. He was indulging her by going to the parade. She could tell he would much rather have kept her in bed for a few more hours doing deliciously naughty things than troop across the city to watch high school marching bands and homemade floats.

Eric raised a questioning eyebrow when she reached under her shirt to stash her money and other things in her bra.

"What? It's not like a pickpocket is getting in there." She picked up the folding chairs she'd found in a storage closet and handed them to Eric. "Here, you can carry these." Once his hands were busy, she plopped a silly green top hat on his head.

"Really?" he groaned.

"You look great!" she told him before wrapping a green feather boa around her neck.

Leia stepped through the front door and waited for Eric to check that the digital lock engaged behind them before they set out for Abercorn Street where they could watch the parade.

They cut down Liberty Street, heading toward the tall spires of the Cathedral. The crisp morning air was refreshing, and the bright sun promised a perfect day for the parade. Eric slung an arm around her shoulder and tucked her against his side as they navigated the busy sidewalks and barricades already in place.

The distraction of the parade was just what she needed, something to take her mind off the questions swirling in her mind about her and Eric.

He was a pragmatist; she was a rule follower. He bent the rules when he needed to reach a goal. The whole Larry situation still made her uncomfortable. Did Eric do it for her, or because that was just what he did? Kidnapping another human being was kind of a big deal to her. That she had been willing to go along with it at all, and even assist, was worrying.

She assumed Eric would have done a similar thing for a regular client. He was willing to step over a lot of lines that Leia saw as uncrossable. If not for that fact, she'd already be planning how to make their relationship work back in New York. *Who am I kidding?* Life upside down and uncomfortable with his job or not, she was falling fast.

They turned left on to Abercorn Street and passed a line of groggy neighbors sharing a thermos of coffee and staking a claim on a parade spot with their lawn chairs.

"See, Eric, we needed to get out here early, or all the good spots would be gone."

He nodded and looked up and down the block. "Okay, you're right, it's getting crowded. Where do you want to be?"

"I guess this is as good a spot as any, and there's a cute café over there. We can grab some breakfast."

They unfolded their chairs and settled in with breakfast sandwiches and coffees from the café.

Waiting for the parade to start was half the fun. Soon they had met the people seated on either side of them. They were all locals from Savannah and had opinions on the best parts of the parade, what bars sold the finest green beer, and which marching band had the worst uniforms.

Watching Eric charm the strangers around them reminded Leia he was nothing like any of the men she'd ever been with—he cast them all in the shade. It wasn't just that he was movie-star handsome. It was the way the air crackled between them when their eyes met, the shock that raced down her spine when his hand touched her skin.

There was something between them that eclipsed chemistry, a connection Leia was learning to crave. Her misgivings about him and the future seemed to be less important than that connection, and it scared her.

While Eric was busy chatting, another of their new acquaintances, a harried mother of a very busy seven- or eight-year-old, leaned close to Leia and asked, "Is he for real?"

"What?" Confused, Leia glanced around, trying to figure out what the woman was asking.

"Your boyfriend, is he for real? Those smoldering glances and that body." The woman waved her hand in front of her face pretending to cool her blushing cheeks. "Whew, girl! Enjoy it. Men like him are a rare find."

Blushing, Leia smiled at the woman before they shared a quick fist bump and giggle. Her new friend pulled out a small flask and passed it over. Leia accepted it and poured a shot into her coffee as she'd seen the woman do minutes before.

"Irish coffee: the official breakfast drink of Savannah." The woman winked.

"Thanks. It looks like it's about to start." Leia took Eric's hand in hers, waiting for the first convertible with the grand marshal to roll past.

The parade was everything she hoped. Eric and Leia abandoned their lawn chairs and joined the locals leaning over the barricades to cheer on the floats and marching bands. The parade may draw in tourists, but it was easy to see it was a glimpse into the tight-knit city of Savannah.

Floats were flatbed trailers and pontoon boats pulled by every kind of truck imaginable. Most of the participants were local Irish families that had been marching for generations. The high school bands came from as far away as Illinois, and even the Clydesdales trotted past.

When the Savannah ladies grabbed Leia and pulled her over the barricades with them, she had no idea what was happening. Until the first one stole a kiss from a soldier of the 3rd Infantry Division as they marched past. The soldiers, from Fort Stewart, were accustomed to the *extra* southern hospitality and didn't even fall out of step as the ladies, including Leia, thanked them for their service with a smooch.

"Should I be jealous?" Eric asked as he lifted her back over the railing and onto the sidewalk. He slid Leia's body down his before her feet touched the pavement, keeping her locked against him.

"Never," she replied, a little breathless, before Eric stole a kiss of his own from her smiling lips.

Reluctantly she pulled back from his embrace. "I need to visit the ladies' room. Want anything from the café?"

"Hold on, I'm coming with." He asked one of their new friends to watch their seats.

Together they walked down the sidewalk to the little café. Outside, a large sign reminded parade-goers that restrooms were for customers only. They joined the short line to reach the order counter and buy a few bottled waters.

"Bathroom?" she asked as Eric took the bottles of water from the cashier.

The woman frantically ringing up customers waved Leia toward a narrow hallway between the two glass coolers that displayed the café's sweet treats and sandwiches. The hallway had a swinging saloon-style door that separated it from the main room.

"I'll be right back," Leia told him before heading down the dim hallway.

The small bathroom was tidy and smelled much better than any of the porta-potties lining the parade route. Glancing in the mirror as Leia washed her hands before leaving, she realized she looked happy. Not just a regular kind of happy but more of the glowing from the inside kind of happy. Strange to think that in the middle of all the upheaval in her life, today she was happy. She gave her green boa a final fluff and unlocked the bathroom door.

The door slammed open, and Max barreled inside. His shoulder slammed into her, dropping her to the ground. Leia slumped onto the linoleum, gasping air back into her lungs. Pain radiated from her bruised ribs, and she wheezed and curled in half.

Before she could get her feet under her and try to stand, rough hands grabbed her upper arms, pulling her up.

Max was bigger than she remembered from the hotel. He pushed her up against the wall, her feet barely skimming the floor. She dangled in front of him, trying to struggle, but he used the length of his body to subdue her as he leaned in close. His hot, humid breath streamed over her face, and he covered her mouth with one hand.

"I've been watching. He's keeping you close." Max's dark eyes were wild, and it looked like he hadn't shaved since DC. An angry gash closed with haphazard sutures sliced through his eyebrow, adding to his terrifying appearance.

Leia struggled, trying to kick or bite. She wished she'd taken a self-defense class.

Max slipped a hypodermic needle from a pocket and jabbed it into her thigh. Instantly she felt like she was underwater, and her struggles slowed as her vision grew hazy. Max dropped his hand from her mouth. She couldn't force a scream.

The attack had taken moments.

Max wrapped an arm around her and half walked half-dragged her through the back door of the café and into a small alleyway. He held her close to his side, and to the world, she looked like she'd had one Irish coffee too many. Her mind slid further into unconsciousness with each step, her head falling forward and her eyes slipping shut.

Leia had no idea how far Max took her, but she was barely lucid when he tipped her into the trunk of his car and zip-tied her ankles and wrists.

The last words Leia heard before slipping into total unconsciousness were, "Let's go see your boss." The thunk of the trunk lid sealed her in darkness.

THE COLD FROM the concrete floor was the first thing to penetrate the fog enveloping Leia's brain. She was uncomfortable and trying to shift, seeking the warmth of Eric's embrace.

Moving was difficult. Her hands were trapped, painfully stuck together. She couldn't get away from the hardness digging into the bones of her shoulder, elbow, and hip. Fighting to open her eyes was exhausting. She wanted to rest but somehow knew she needed to wake up.

A loud grinding and then the low hum of a big engine filled the space around Leia. Her teeth rattled and a headache pounded behind her closed eyes. Again she tried to shift, move to a more comfortable position that might protect her from the loud noise, but pain seared her wrists and her feet refused to cooperate.

Finally, she peeled her gritty eyelids open. Bright light burned her eyes. Her tangled hair obscured her view, but through the strands, she tried to focus on her surroundings. The space was a vast open warehouse with corrugated metal walls and polished concrete floors. She was lying in the farthest corner, and across from her, a massive rolling door had just opened to let in the midday sun. A sleek private jet was pulling to a stop in the center of the hanger.

Leia looked down to see that black zip ties encircled her wrists and ankles, cutting cruelly into her skin when she would pull against them. Her body ached from the manhandling, and fear crept up her spine: Max. He did this to her, drugged her, brought her here.

It came flooding back—the parade, the attack in the bathroom, Max drugging her before he shoved her in the trunk of a car. She was trapped.

Leia heard the muffled steps of rubber-soled combat boots before Max's legs blocked her view. He used the toe of his boot to push her face up so he could look at her.

"Good, you're awake. About fucking time." He yanked his foot away from her jaw, letting her head thump back on the ground. He knelt by her feet; a knife flashed in his hand seconds before it sliced through the ties on her ankles. Rolling Leia flat on her back, his hands roamed over her body, touching—searching.

Panic gripped her heart. Clothes offered no shield from his touch. Tears were gathering. She barely had the strength to keep her eyes open much less to fight his assault.

His hands paused over her left breast at the crinkling of paper. He slipped his hand inside her bra and withdrew a few twenties and a scrap of white paper. Standing over Leia, he unfolded the note; a manic smile spread over his face when he read it.

"The cell number on this paper, it's Eric's cell, isn't it? I know this is his handwriting. He must be worried about you by now." Max slipped the cash and paper into his pocket before dragging her up by one arm.

The room spun under her feet, dizziness and nausea from the drugs overwhelming her and forcing her to cling to Max. He let her stumble along beside him until they were at the base of the jet's gangway.

Max tugged brutally on Leia's hair, pulling her head up so she could watch Sal Marino make his way down from the plane. The pain radiating from her scalp was nothing compared to the brutal slap Sal delivered when he came to a stop in front of them. The large gold college ring he wore split open her lip on impact.

The rusty taste of blood filled her mouth. The urge to heave was strong, she fought down the bile rising up the back of her throat. Max let go of her hair, and her head slumped forward. Silent tears slid down her cheeks and mixed with the blood, leaving red drops on the gray concrete floor by her feet and splashing on her white running shoes.

"Stupid girl! You have caused me an unending amount of problems." Sal was livid. The mild-mannered accountant persona had dissolved, revealing a mobster bent on revenge. "Going to the FBI. You think we don't know? Do you think Eric Robb can protect you from our organization? We've been watching you. Poor choice to visit our bank in Savannah. We monitor the security cameras closely."

Held in place by Max and with blood already dripping down her face, she begged Sal Marino for her life.

"Sal, please," she sobbed. "I can get it back. I can get it all back. The FBI doesn't believe me. They think I made it up."

She'd never been this scared in her life. She was hysterical, hyperventilating between her gasped pleas. She hated her weakness, but she was desperate to live. "Give me twenty-four hours. I can make it right. Please." She struggled to hold herself up. Fear and desperation made her feel heavy like she was going to crumple onto the floor.

"There is no making it right. There is only you paying for your mistake," Sal said.

He was issuing her death sentence. The future her father dreamed of for her would never come to pass. Her life would be coming to a painfully bitter end.

"I am sorry, God, I'm so sorry. I wish I'd never found that stupid bank. Stolen those files." Sobs racked her body, and she trembled in Max's grasp.

"Leia, there is no apologizing for what you did. The good news for us is no one will miss you when you're gone."

Images of Eric from the last few days flooded her mind: that morning at the parade, laughing at dinner their first night in Savannah, his head bending for a goodnight kiss. He'd been so determined to help her. He'd blame himself for her disappearance and, ultimately, her death. It wasn't fair; they'd only just met.

"Max, you need to go clean up the Robb mess," Sal said.

"Don't worry. Eric Robb won't leave Savannah alive."

All of this was her fault.

She was sobbing hard; Max shook her and growled under his breath, telling her to shut up.

"Should I just dump this one's body in the swamp on the way back to town?" Max asked, clearly annoyed with her crying.

"No, don't kill her. She's worth something to Oblonsky. I owe him after this shit show." Sal was matter of fact, discussing Leia's life like a change in the weather. "Don't worry. You'll still get paid on both contracts."

Hearing her fate would be in the hands of Pavel Oblonsky was enough to send a fresh round of tremors through Leia's body. A sob lodged in her throat, choking her, and tears slid down her face unchecked.

The sound of squealing tires interrupted the conversation. A black Range Rover pulled into the hanger and came to a stop alongside the jet. When the car door slammed closed, Leia struggled to lift her head to see. A young man got out. He was tall and broad. He looked like a soldier, even had a holster with a gun strapped to his shoulder. Thick black Cyrillic tattoos trailed up his bare arms. He leaned against the driver's side quarter panel of the pretentious SUV, arms crossed.

"Ya, I am here for Mr. Oblonsky." His Russian accent was heavy, his English clumsy.

"Good, he should be right out. You want the girl drugged again?" Sal asked.

"Nyet."

Thankful there would be no more drugs injected into her body, Leia let her head fall back down and stared at her shoes. She was desperately trying to think of a way out, a way to get free. Then she smelled it—the cloying musk of Oblonsky's cologne. The same scent he wore for his meeting at Marino & Associates last week. It was enough to send her falling to her knees, her stomach spasming. She managed not to vomit, but a cold sweat bathed her body.

Oblonsky chuckled as he descended the gangway. "Ah, my reputation precedes me. She is already on her knees. Fast learner this whore."

Leia stole a glance. Oblonsky reminded her of a bull with his large build and flat nose. Today a dark blood red shirt strained across his chest, the neck open to reveal a thick gold cross tangled in his graying chest hair. He wore a holster like the driver's that he was in the process of covering with a black suit jacket. His expensive shoes clicked on the gangway steps.

"She's all yours, Pavel. Kill her if she isn't useful. Can't let her rat anyone else out," Sal said.

"She will work until she is used up. She is young enough to earn me something for all this trouble. Used up women either kill themselves or fade out of existence. Don't worry about this one anymore." Oblonsky stepped past Leia without a backward glance and barked an order in Russian to the driver.

The burly driver stepped forward, reached down for Leia, and tossed her over his shoulder like a side of beef. His thick shoulder dug into her stomach and bruised her tender ribs with each long step he took. When he dumped her in the back of the Range Rover, he quickly taped her ankles and mouth with straps of wide silver-tape before he carelessly tossed a blanket over her body.

Max was hunting Eric, and she was at the mercy of Pavel Oblonsky. Her perfect day at the parade had turned into a living nightmare. She curled under the blanket in the back of the SUV. The two men in the front seat ignored her quiet weeping.

"LEIA?" Eric answered when he snatched up the ringing cell phone from the table. He was sitting at a table in the Savannah City Market. He'd been fighting the St Patrick's Day crowds for hours, searching the two and a half square miles that were downtown Savannah, hoping to find her. Her green feather boa left in the café's alleyway was all he had recovered.

"Nope, it's just me, partner, but if you want your pretty little accountant back, we need to meet." Max's voice was cheerful. Money was the only thing he ever took seriously. That had always pissed Eric off.

"Is she alive?"

"For now. Fifteen minutes at the Waving Girl Statue on the waterfront."

The line clicked dead in Eric's hand. He bolted from the table. It was less than a mile to the statue, but a sea of people celebrating St Patrick's Day stood between him and his destination.

He elbowed his way through the worst congestion in the City Market area, heading cross-town. He broke into a full run when he could and dodged cars and drunk tourists on the streets. His feet ate up the pavement. Every bar or restaurant that fronted on the sidewalk caused a human traffic jam he had to break through. Cold beer sloshed down his arm, drenching his sleeve; he didn't slow down to apologize. Behind him, an angry college kid chucked his now-empty plastic cup at Eric's back.

Half a mile later, slowing to a brisk walk, Eric tried to catch his breath, the crowds of partiers almost non-existent here at the unpopular end of the waterfront. The sun was setting, and a ring of trees cast long shadows around the edge of the park where the statue stood. It made him nervous. Checking his watch, he was three minutes early. It felt like a setup. It would be foolish to just stroll into the open grass around the statue.

His senses were on high alert as he crept to a bench under one of the large trees with a brick retaining wall at his back. It felt wrong—the park, the deserted open space. It was cold sitting on the bench in the shade. Night was approaching fast. He could smell the brackish water of the Savannah River. A city-operated ferry boat chugged slowly past, the voices of its passengers carrying over the water. The ferry was slowing to dock just at the end of the park.

Eric moved along the perimeter of the park, staying in the shadows of the trees. The ferry's arrival was too perfect. *Max must be on the boat.* Eric leaned against an oak. Although he was far from the dock, he could make out the people as they got ready to disembark. Max was big, linebacker big; he should be easy to spot.

Flipping open the blade on his folding tactical knife, Eric wished he had a gun, but bringing a concealed firearm to a parade had seemed like an excellent way to get arrested. The weight of the knife was familiar; he'd carried it for years. It would have to do. He kept the blade pressed into the folds of his pants, down and out of sight.

The crowd on the boat was shuffling off the gangway, corralled by a boat captain through a series of railing switchbacks, bottlenecked and only able to move as fast as the person in front of them. Just stepping into the maze of railings was Max, and more than a dozen slow-moving passengers were in front of and behind him.

Eric dashed onto the quay, hopped one of the metal railings, and wedged himself behind Max. He wrapped Max in a one-armed bear hug to disguise his knife pressing against Max's back. Max looked rough: a patchy beard, ugly stitches over one eye, and a dirty cast on his right wrist. Even his clothes were sloppy.

"Max, my old friend, how you been?" Eric slurred loudly, smiling at the tourists he'd jostled when he leapt into line. Everyone loves a friendly drunk.

Eric stayed close and slid his hand under Max's shirt, where he found a compact handgun tucked in the small of his back. Eric palmed the gun and dropped it in his pocket.

"Where is Leia?" Eric asked.

"Not here."

The line of passengers kept shuffling forward. Eric dug the tip of the knife into the flesh over Max's ribs. Max sucked in a hard breath, otherwise ignoring the pain.

"Where is she?" Eric pushed the blade deeper.

"Not here," Max grunted.

As the passengers exited the line, most turned right toward the waterfront. There was a small blonde woman between Max and the end of the aisle. Eric tried to secure his hold on Max, but the bigger man turned his upper body away from the knife and dropped his right shoulder to lay down a tackle that put Eric on his ass. He tumbled backward into the people in line, caught in a tangle of limbs.

Max barreled through the little blonde lady without pausing, sprinting away from the quay toward the water-front crowds. Eric tracked Max's path with his eyes. Regaining his feet, he leapt over the little blonde and dashed after Max. Eric had always been the faster runner; he hoped he still was.

He hurried across the open park, heading for River Street. Following Max in the crowd was surprisingly easy. Max was making no effort at stealth, tackling and shoving people out of his way, using his size to make a hole. Eric slowly gained on him despite the crowd, and soon he could see Max a few yards ahead of him.

With a loud crash, a rack of postcards at a souvenir stand exploded into the air as Max shoved it out of his way and ducked off the main drag into the alley that ran behind River Street. Eric followed, gaining with every stride.

Eric rounded the corner behind Max. The alley was part of the old Factors Walk, and the uneven cobblestones under his feet sloped upward sharply. He slowed his pace to avoid falling or twisting an ankle in the dark. The lights from the businesses' service entrances cast a pale glow, illuminating dumpsters and parked cars. On his left was a twenty-foot tall stone wall, the remnants of the historic cotton market, boxing in the alley. Their footsteps echoed in the cavern-like space.

Max was slowing; Eric surged forward to tackle the bigger man to the ground. Max took the brunt of the fall, his arm with the cast crashing into the cobblestones. They grappled, and Max caught Eric's right hand, the knife suspended between the two men.

"Tell me where Leia is, Max."

"Fuck you."

Eric leaned all his weight on his right arm, the knife-point dipping toward Max's chest.

Max growled, bucking his body up, twisting, throwing Eric to the side. The knife fell from Eric's hand and clattered across the cobblestones. They both jumped to their feet.

"I can pay you more than the contract."

"It's not about money. I want to kill you." Max's voice was breaking, bordering on hysterical.

"Revenge?"

"No, a reckoning."

Eric could see that Max was distraught, beyond what he would expect in the heat of the moment.

"They told me to kill you." Max continued ranting gibberish about death and the reckoning, crossing over. None of it made any sense to Eric.

Eric had no idea who *they* were, but he didn't think it was Sal Marino. Who else would want him dead and have Max worked into such a rage?

Eric stepped forward, looking for an opening to throw a punch. Max swung; Eric dodged the blow. They had sparred for years. Both were good with their fists. Max had power because of his size, but a broken arm should minimize his wicked right hook. They traded body blows, then Eric swung hard, connecting with Max's head and reopening the sutures over his eyebrow.

"You're too late anyway. By now that Russian, Oblonsky, has probably passed her around to a dozen paying clients."

Eric never understood the expression *seeing red* until now. Rage unlike any he'd ever felt burned through his body. Oblonsky had Leia. His fists flew with a strength he didn't know he possessed, striking Max with the force of a sledgehammer. The larger man staggered back, wiping blood from his eyes.

"Hey! What the hell is going on down there?" The blinding beam of a Maglite swept the sunken alley from above. Looking down on them from one of the many catwalks that stretched over the Factors Walk was a Savannah city cop.

"Freeze!" the cop yelled.

Max took off running, heading off into the darkness. Eric turned on his heel and opened the closest service door, stepping into a busy kitchen.

Not a single person working in the chaotic kitchen turned their head when Eric stepped in from the alley. The line cooks and dishwashers looked like they were in the heat of battle. Sweat poured off the men, pots clanged, and grill fires flared. At the pass window, a woman in chef's whites barked orders like an admiral on the deck of a warship. Behind her, waitstaff dressed in all black hustled plates out to the dining room.

Eric hung back near the door to the alley; he was breathing hard from the fight. He straightened his clothes, smoothed his hair, and wiped the sweat off his face. The bright kitchen lights let him inspect his split knuckles and scraped palms.

He shifted his body, feeling the pain in his ribs and back from Max's punches. He leaned back against the wall. He could be mistaken for a waiter on a smoke break if someone didn't look too close.

Leia was in trouble and needed his help. If she were swallowed up by Oblonsky's organization, he would never locate her. Trafficked women just disappeared. He replayed the fight in his head, Max's strange behavior, his references to *they*. None of it would help him find Leia.

Fear had started gnawing a hole in his gut; he needed a lead. Max was in the wind, leaving Eric burning with impotent fury. The email he sent to Simms was still unanswered, so he couldn't count on help from the Feds either.

"Hey, asshole! Get to work." One of the line cooks pointed a spoon at him. "No breaks during the rush."

Eric hung his head, hoping none of the staff would notice he was a stranger, and started for the front of the kitchen. He was weaving his way toward the exit the other waiters were using, ducking out of the way of trays and hot pans.

Long fingers wrapped around Eric's bicep. The chef tugged him close and hissed, "Who the hell are you?" Caught, Eric took the tray with a beautiful plate of fish in cream sauce on it that she shoved at him. "Never mind, I don't fucking care who you are, run this to table twelve." She pushed him none too gently toward the kitchen door.

Eric stumbled out the door in the wake of a waitress. He reached out and tapped the woman on the shoulder. When she turned to face him, he shrugged in confusion and asked, "Table twelve?"

She scowled and pointed him to a table on the left before rushing toward her customers. The restaurant was white tablecloths and fresh flowers, expensive and packed to the gills.

As Eric set the plate in front of the older lady at the table, she looked up, smiled, and asked, "Is it fresh off the boat today?"

"Yes…" Something clicked in Eric's brain when he heard the word boat. "The Narcissus."

Holy fuck! Eric had his lead. He knew where Oblonsky was tonight, thanks to Larry from the *Gas N Go*: the port in Brunswick.

Tray still in hand, Eric ran for the front of the restaurant, his sprint across the formal room attracting more than one glare. He dropped the tray on the hostess stand as he jogged past, then shoved his way out of the restaurant's doors, right into a high-end hotel lobby.

A large green and gold banner overhead proclaimed the Shamrock Ball; it hung above a red carpet leading to a ballroom glowing with green lights. Eric jumped over the velvet rope and raced for the hotel's open front door.

The VIP valet parking line was backing up River Street. There had to be a dozen luxury cars waiting for parking attendants to snag the keys from the *very important* drivers so they could waltz into the ball.

Eric sized up the options: fight both human and vehicle traffic to get back to the carriage house and the Jaguar on the other side of town or help the valet parkers with their backup. He had no idea what time Oblonsky would be at the port, but it was already seven o'clock, and Brunswick was over an hour away. Every second counted. He needed a car now.

He stepped up to the valet stand and grabbed a discarded ticket book off the top. Casually, he walked around to open the driver side door of the blacked-out matte finish Audi R8 that had just rolled to the front of the line. This car could undeniably get him to the port in under an hour.

The purr of the supercar's powerful engine almost drowned out Eric's greeting. "Hello, sir. Welcome to the Shamrock Ball. Don't forget your ticket." He passed a parking stub to the man in a tux with a green bow tie.

Eric slid into the driver's seat; a beautiful blonde woman was still sitting in the passenger seat, wearing a daring silver evening gown. She devoured Eric's body with her eyes while she finished touching up her blood-red lipstick. Her perfectly manicured hand dropped on the top of Eric's leg.

"Don't hurt the car. He loves it more than me," the icy beauty purred while squeezing Eric's thigh. She turned and accepted her date's assistance in getting out of the low-slung car, the door closing behind her.

Eric eased the car out of the valet line and asked the

hands-free navigation system to find the fastest route to the Port of Brunswick.

He wove his way across the downtown streets. The traffic was still unwinding from the parade, but a blatant disregard for traffic laws helped him clear the city quickly.

The Audi was savagely fast and responded like a race car. He effortlessly broke seventy miles per hour accelerating up the highway on-ramp. Flying down I-95, Eric ducked around slow-moving minivans and tractor-trailers, pushing the car's limits as he headed south to the port. Speed limits were for other people; his only concern was finding Leia.

SIXTEEN

EXITING I-95, Eric slowed the Audi to the speed limit. The entrance to the port was a few miles from the off-ramp. A gas station and a few fast-food restaurants crowded near the highway, but beyond them, there was nothing along the two-lane road that wound through the coastal marshland to the port.

Minutes later, sitting at the traffic light for the port entrance, Eric saw a line of empty tractor-trailers waiting to pass through security before they could enter the port and pick up their newly arrived shipping containers. There were at least a few dozen trucks stacked up under the yellow glow of sodium vapor lights. At the front of the line, flanked by a tall chain-link fence and concrete barriers, was a small security booth with the Homeland Security logo.

The light turned green, and Eric eased the car through the intersection. Across the road was a stand of pine trees. Stunted from the exposure to the salty ocean air, they huddled along the outside of the port's security fence. Once across the intersection, Eric flipped a quick U-turn, easing the Audi onto the gravel shoulder.

He cringed as the car's undercarriage scraped over the uneven ground. The low-profile Audi barely made it up and over the roadside ditch that separated the stand of trees from the shoulder. He parked under the branches of the pine trees, and the black car melted into the darkness when he flipped off the headlights.

Eric sat in the car, dropped his head to the steering wheel, and closed his eyes. This was his best chance at finding Oblonsky and a lead on Leia's whereabouts. If Oblonsky had already left with his container, Eric was at a dead-end; even the FBI would have a hard time finding her once she fell into the hellish world of human trafficking.

Max's 9mm sat in the seat next to him. Eric checked to see it was fully loaded, and then the small handgun went into a deep pocket on his pants. The weapon was all he had; his favorite knife was lying in a Savannah alley. A pair of leather driving gloves in the center console caught his eye, and he shoved them into another pocket. His quick search of the glove box yielded nothing helpful.

Even with limited resources, getting into a port known as the vehicle import center of the Eastern seaboard shouldn't be insurmountable. Eric took the Audi's key fob with him and ducked out of the car.

From the deep shadows under the pine trees, he watched the security procedures for entry. It was mostly a formality with a tubby guard in a blue uniform talking to the truck driver, checking identification and paperwork. There was no vehicle inspection.

On the other hand, the chain-link fence Eric was looking through was about twelve feet high and topped off with what looked like newly installed razor wire. Scaling it wouldn't be an option, and with no tools, cutting a hole was even less likely.

Walking down the fence line toward the main road, he

clung to the shadows. He ducked around the end and walked back toward the row of waiting trucks. The shadows from the trees were interrupted by the occasional glow from an overhead lamppost, the yellow light not penetrating far in the thick darkness.

The weak point in the security check was the trailer; he would use that to get through the gate.

Stopped in a dark spot between overhead lights, the fifth truck in line looked like Eric's best option. The driver in the semi behind number five wasn't paying attention to anything, his face buried in the glow from his cell phone. Eric should be able to dart out of the shadows and dive under number five's trailer without anyone noticing.

He bolted, sliding under the trailer like he was stealing third base. The frame above his head was a lattice of trusses, the dark metal cold and greasy. He pulled the driving gloves on, hoping they might help his grip. He threaded his arms and legs around the cross pieces, wedging his shoulder and hip up into the undercarriage to help support his weight.

Hanging, waiting for the truck to lurch forward every time it advanced in line, he forced himself to relax. Letting the adrenaline take over would be a mistake. Calm and focused, he was like ice in the field. No formal military training, but his retired military father had drilled him since he was a kid on how to handle pressure. From hunting and sports to school work, Eric's father had trained him to concentrate like his life depended on it. Tonight it wasn't just his life, but Leia's as well.

The truck sped up, no longer just the idle roll that had advanced it through the line at the checkpoint. He hugged the metal cross piece tight, pulling himself up against the frame. A speed bump or other obstacle in the roadway could be deadly if he hung too far below the undercarriage.

He choked back a cough from the road dust and exhaust fumes filling his nose.

The semi rolled along one of the roads in the port, winding farther from the security booth. He had little choice but to hang on and go where it went. A few minutes after clearing the entrance, the truck slowed, and Eric heard the truck's air brakes engage when the driver came to a complete stop.

Around the semi, it appeared dark, so he dropped from his perch and belly crawled out from under the trailer to take a look. The truck was again waiting in a line, but now it was well inside the port. Looking up, he could see that the lights atop the enormous ship-to-shore cranes at the water's edge were close.

Once clear of the trailer, Eric stood and scanned the area; a few hundred feet away, there were a series of low office buildings. A small well-lit sign on top said Marine Terminal Office. Keeping to the shadows, he headed toward the offices.

The cheap lock on the outside door put up little resistance, popping open when he rammed it with his shoulder. Inside the offices, it was the standard layout of desks with aging computer work stations. He selected one at the back of the room and flipped on the CPU tower and screen.

While he waited for the machine to turn on, Eric explored the office. On the back wall near an exit door, he found a row of hooks with hard hats and safety vests; he put on one of each. Blending in was always better than sneaking around.

He perched gingerly on the edge of the ancient office chair at the desk, his every movement causing the vinyl to squeal. The noise was deafening in the silent room. The computer was finally booted up.

The software for the port required a login.

"Fuck," he muttered, running a hand over his face. He could hack the system, but it would take time.

He opened the desk drawer, searching for any clue to the password. An ID badge on a lanyard, right on top, gave him a name to work from.

He looked at the time on the computer display; it was after nine o'clock. He needed to get to work.

As he let his fingers rest on the dingy keyboard, he looked down at the ID on the desk. In the picture was a blue-collar looking guy with a beard. He had to be over fifty. Not exactly the kind of guy to be overly concerned with computer security.

Eric picked up the keyboard. Bingo!

There was a row of pink post-it notes stuck to the Formica desktop. One was helpfully labeled with the name of the port program and had both username and password. There was one with an email account password and the last with a Facebook login.

The port program was pretty basic, looked like it hadn't been upgraded since Y2K twenty years ago. He found a search by function and typed in *Narcissus*.

The record for the ship opened—she was in port and scheduled for unloading all night at dock 7-B.

Standing, he grabbed the lanyard and pulled it over his neck. The ID may not look like him, but it was better than nothing. Before walking out of the busted door, he stopped and swept his eyes over the office one last time. Next to the safety vests on the back wall was a poster-size map of the Marine Terminal. He snapped a quick cell phone photo for reference and shoved a clipboard under his arm.

Seeming annoyed and carrying a clipboard was key to looking like you belonged in a place like this.

Eric left the office building behind, taking a direct route to dock 7-B. He hoped he would be in time to find Oblonsky and Larry.

"HEY, HEY, MAN! WAIT UP," yelled the security guard in a four-seater utility vehicle that looked like a cross between a pickup truck and a golf cart on steroids. He pulled alongside Eric. "Need a ride?"

"Uhm, sure." Eric sat in the passenger seat. The hike to the Narcissus didn't look that far on the map, but the scale of the port was impressive. "Heading to dock 7-B."

"Yeah, I figured. There's only two ships unloading tonight. My name's Nelson." The guard awkwardly stuck his left hand over the steering wheel to shake.

"I'm Bill." Eric figured he could use the name on the stolen ID; it was better than nothing.

Nelson pushed the accelerator down, and the cart cruised past darkened buildings and acres of new cars fresh off the boat from Europe and still wrapped in protective plastic. The cold sea air whipped past Eric's face as they barreled down the path toward another set of ship-to-shore cranes that were lifting the containers from the deck of the Narcissus and onto the waiting tractor-trailers lined up along the quay.

"You heading down to the trucks or need to go up with the crane operators?"

Eric looked at the platform that was a few flights of metal stairs above the pavement. "Up there will work. Thanks for the ride." He patted Nelson on the shoulder as he got out of the cart.

He pounded up the three flights of stairs to an extended platform that connected the bases of the three ship-to-shore cranes used for unloading at dock 7-B. From the main level, a crane operator would climb up more flights of stairs to access their crane's steering control booth. Eric walked to the center of the platform to an observation stand. He nudged the mouse on the computer that sat on the work desk, waking it up.

Scanning the dock, he watched as one of the massive cranes that was above his head plucked a container from the Narcissus and gently set it down on the waiting trailer. The semi driver waited for it to be locked into place and then received the all-clear to pull out, joining the line of trucks waiting to leave the port.

A pair of expensive top-of-the-line German optical binoculars sat on the desk; he used them to scan the rest of the quay. From his post on the platform, the people down by the ship looked like ants without the field glasses.

Far to the right, there was a holding area with a handful of empty tractor-trailers waiting to pick up their loads. The drivers were standing under a light post hanging out. A white puff of vapor from an e-cigarette flashed, catching his attention when he passed the binoculars over the group. The cloud cleared from the smoker's face and revealed the gold-toothed smile of his new best buddy Larry. The German binoculars were so strong Eric could see Larry was still wearing a bandaid on the tip of his pinky finger. He couldn't help but smile.

He scanned the rest of the area before he found Oblonsky—or at least what he assumed was him. A heavily chromed black Range Rover with the interior lights on idled in a shadowy storage yard bordering the port exit road. Inside the SUV, Eric could see two men with their heads bent close in conversation.

He wasn't too late. He had a location for Oblonsky.

Eric swiveled his attention back to the drivers. Larry took a final toke off his e-cig and left the others, heading for a new white Peterbilt. The small man clambered into the driver's seat and moved his semi into the line for the second crane.

Racing down the metal stairs, Eric dashed from the crane platform and circled behind a row of stacked containers. He jogged to the far end, sticking to the shadows. The Range Rover was parked a few hundred feet away across the open pavement from where Eric crouched. He couldn't chance running toward the SUV; he would spook Oblonsky.

Looking back toward the ship, Eric watched as the second crane plucked a forty-foot-long red container from the Narcissus and maneuvered it over Larry's trailer. The ground crew stepped up and locked it into place, giving Larry the go-ahead signal minutes later.

The doors on the Rover popped open, and from his position, Eric could only see the man getting out on the driver's side. The guy was a giant. Well over six feet of brute strength. Must be Oblonsky's muscle. The guy walked to the back of the car, and the tailgate opened. Light from inside the vehicle spilled out, illuminating two figures behind the Rover. The driver and Oblonsky. Oblonsky wasn't as big as his driver or as fit, but he was still a mountain of a man. Eric knew it was him from the photos he'd seen on the web.

The white Peterbilt crawled up to the SUV, stopping with the back of the trailer parallel to the open tailgate.

The driver reached into the back of the SUV with both arms and pulled out something wrapped in a blue tarp. Suddenly the tarp moved, and part of a woman's arm and a fall of dark hair spilled out.

Eric's heart stopped. *Leia?*

Oblonsky reached out and tugged the tarp away from her face before delivering a vicious backhand. He wrapped his fingers around her slender throat. Eric couldn't hear what the man said, but it must have been a brutal threat. Leia shrunk into the driver's chest, trying to get away from Oblonsky. Eric's stomach clenched with suppressed rage, his calm, calculating focus burning up.

Juggling Leia in his arms, the driver tugged the tarp back over her. Together the men hurried to the back of the stopped semi. Oblonsky efficiently opened the latches on the rear of the container, just cracking the door. The driver stepped up and thrust Leia into the blackness before sealing the doors again. Seeing Leia treated like another piece of meat for the sex trade made Eric want to rip Oblonsky apart with his bare hands.

The Peterbilt pulled out of the meeting area, rolling toward the line of tractor-trailers waiting to clear the port. Oblonsky and his driver got back in the SUV and followed the semi.

SEVENTEEN

PAIN SHOT up Leia's arm when her shoulder hit the shipping container's hard metal floor. She fought up to sitting, spinning around, trying to reach the door before it was closed again. The loud bang as it shut reverberated in the hollow space.

Her eyes slowly adjusted to the low LED lighting inside the steel box. Around her, there were twenty or thirty young women. Most sat huddled together on makeshift beds with their backs resting on the container walls; they were obviously scared.

The foul scent of unwashed bodies and human waste burned the back of Leia's throat. She could see blankets hung at the end of the container, she assumed to hide a crude toilet. Wrappers from junk food and energy bars littered the ground.

One of the women crawled forward. She held out her hands, palms up, reaching toward Leia's bound wrists. Leia extended her arms, and the woman used a blunt knife to sever the ties. Burning pain accompanied the blood that rushed back to her fingers. She held back a sob, rubbing her hands together. When her hands had feeling back, Leia ripped the tape from her lips. The pain was worth it. She could breathe freely again.

The woman went to work on Leia's bound ankles. The bouncing and swaying of the truck reminded her they were moving. Once Leia's ankles were free, the woman moved back to her space on the wall and gestured for her to do the same.

Leia moved next to the woman. "Do you speak English?"

"Very little."

Her heavy accent sounded Eastern European. The woman was young, maybe even a teenager. Her stringy hair might be blonde when it was clean.

"Thank you." Leia indicated her unbound limbs.

"Pozhaluysta. What date is this day?" she asked.

"March seventeenth."

The woman nodded her thanks and tried not to cry.

"How long?" Leia asked.

"Thirteen days." The woman closed her eyes and rested her head back on the wall before telling the other women in their language what Leia had said.

In the container, the captive women accepted the news with a mixture of silence and quiet tears.

The young woman's hand was on the floor between them; she slid it over and placed it on top of Leia's, threading their fingers together.

"Do you want to know where you are?"

"No, I already know this is Hell," the woman replied before turning to face Leia. Hopelessness and defeat so powerful Leia could feel them in her soul poured from the captive woman.

Leia drew her knees to her chest, dropped her head down, and she clung to the other woman's hand. Her sobs filled the container. The woman was right. This was Hell.

EIGHTEEN

ERIC RAN like his life depended on it. Seeing Leia helpless in the huge man's arms was more painful than any of the punches Max landed in the alley tonight. He needed to reach the Audi. Getting to the car and following Larry's truck was his priority. His burning lungs, racing heart, and even the ache radiating out of his bad knee were all unimportant.

He needed to cross a large storage lot for newly imported European cars and climb the port's perimeter fence. He raced between the plastic-wrapped vehicles, the blacktop under his feet even and well maintained. The scale of everything at the port was massive; the parking lot he was running across would eclipse ones at shopping malls or football stadiums. Lungs burning, he pushed on.

Row after row of new cars stretched out around him as he ran. He sucked in huge gulps of chilly ocean air laced with exhaust fumes from the semis. He passed between the vehicles, running hard. Off to his right, a line of trucks waited to enter the port, the low rumble of the engines reaching him even over his harsh breathing.

At the end of this row of cars, Eric saw the gleam of the razor wire atop the port's perimeter fence. He turned and followed along the barrier, running toward a ninety-degree corner in the fencing up ahead.

Stopping at the corner in the fence, he looked up. There was a small gap in the razor wire at the top, and the corner post had extra brackets he would be able to utilize as hand and footholds.

He pulled the grimy driving gloves out of his pocket, tugging them on. The thin leather would be some protection for his hands. He pulled off the orange safety vest he was still wearing, wadded it up, and wrapped it around his right hand as an extra layer of defense against the sharp wire.

Climbing the fence should have been easy, but fatigue from the sprint across the storage yard left him breathing hard and his legs like rubber. At the top of the twelve-foot-tall fence, he carefully wedged his shoulders into the gap in the razor wire. A dangerous coil of wire rubbed against him on either side as he balanced on the corner post, wriggling his leg over the top.

Straddling the fence, he twisted so he could pull his second leg over. Finding footholds, he started to climb down, but the coil of razor wire on his right side grabbed his shirt, cutting into his upper arm and shoulder. Cursing under his breath at the pain, he froze.

Fuck, he needed to untangle himself.

Working with his left hand, Eric removed each bit of cloth and skin caught in the vicious metal teeth; by the time he worked himself free, his left hand was dripping blood. Thankfully, he was now clear of the sharp points and could keep climbing down the fence.

When his feet hit the ground, he tugged off the blood-soaked driving glove and looked at his left hand; it was a mess. He bandaged it with the safety vest, doing what he could to staunch the bleeding, and broke into a fast jog.

Cutting through the dark scrub heading toward the main road was slow going, but he could see the glow from the port entrance, he was close. The stand of stunted pines that hid the Audi was ahead, outlined against the horizon.

He couldn't fail Leia; his last memory of her wouldn't be watching her be tossed into a shipping container. The last hundred feet, he ran flat out, stumbling in the darkness. He had to find Oblonsky and Larry before they were lost in the never-ending flow of southbound traffic heading into Florida on I-95.

His heart was racing as he pulled open the door to the Audi and pressed the start button. He wouldn't think about life without Leia. He took a steadying breath, then put the car in gear and crept back out to the main road, searching for the white Peterbilt and black Range Rover in the darkness of the Georgia marshland.

Eric left the exit to the port behind. The two-lane road back to I-95 unfurled into the inky Georgia night. Across the open marshland, Eric could see the distinctive orange running lights outlining the profile of the Range Rover. Oblonsky and Larry were far ahead.

He downshifted the R8 and rammed the accelerator to the floor. The supercar launched forward, devouring the pavement. The small road was dark and curvy, and the only other traffic were trucks heading to and from the port.

He feathered the break as he slid through a corner, accelerating around a slow-moving semi. He flexed the fingers of his left hand; the wheel was sticky with drying blood. Rounding another curve, he slowed, drifting into the opposite lane, waiting for the apex of the corner before redlining the engine again.

In seconds, the car was again trapped behind a

lumbering tractor-trailer. Eric swerved to look around the truck in front of him. Once he passed this truck, there was a long straightaway where he could push the Audi to its limits and eat up the distance between him and Leia.

In the oncoming lane, a convoy of three semi-trucks barreled toward him. He was in their lane, ready to make the pass, but for an instant, he second-guessed the distance, second-guessed the speed of the car, and lifted his right foot from the gas.

No. This isn't the time to second-guess. He slammed his foot back on the accelerator, gritting his teeth. He let the six hundred horsepower engine rocket the Audi through the gap between the massive trucks. The turbulence from the close call with the oncoming tractor-trailers pushed the Audi toward the shoulder, but Eric clutched the wheel with both hands to regain control, his injured hand throbbing in protest. He muttered a curse.

The insignificance of the high-powered sports car in comparison to the semi's massive size hit home. He could catch Larry and Oblonsky, but he couldn't stop them alone.

Holding the car steady with his injured hand, he dug out Simms's business card from his wallet. He dialed the cell number via the handsfree system.

A half-asleep agent Simms answered, "Simms, who is this?"

"Eric Robb. I came in with Leia Stone last week in DC. And sent you an email with more information Monday."

"We are working on verifying—"

He cut off Simms. "Listen. I can help you make the biggest bust of your career. I just need a roadblock."

"What the hell are you and that girl involved with?"

Eric launched into a quick recap of Leia's disappearance and what he saw at the port.

"I'm in an R8, plenty of horsepower to chase down Oblonsky but zero stopping power up against his Range Rover or the semi. I can't even tail them long term. This car is too distinctive. I need that roadblock." He downshifted again as he came out of the long straightaway. He estimated that he would catch up to Oblonsky about the moment they hit the I-95 on-ramp.

"An R what? Never mind. What's in the container?"

"I never saw, but the fact that Oblonsky met it personally at the port makes my best guess women."

"Shit. I'll see what I can do, but with no evidence or advance warning—"

"You have the evidence in that email." Eric was furious. This was why he worked alone. His pulse raced, anger clouding his desire to reason with the agent. The FBI had to help. He had to save Leia. He wouldn't contemplate losing her this way.

"I'm working to verify…"

Eric cursed under his breath. The FBI wasn't turning out to be the lifeline he needed.

"Yeah, I heard you the first time. Look, my intel says they're heading for Jacksonville. Call me back if you can get me an assist." Fuck the FBI. He would do it alone.

"Robb, don't get yourself killed playing chicken on I-95 with a Mack truck."

He clicked off the phone call. He was about to reach the little bit of civilization there was out here—a few gas stations and a Dairy Queen. He slowed down. Not far ahead, the truck and SUV made their way onto I-95 south.

Coasting into town at a hundred miles per hour wasn't smart. The last thing he needed was local law enforcement trying to pull him over.

Actually... Local law enforcement was exactly what he needed. Screw the FBI. His mind flooded with scenarios, and the only good outcomes he could imagine involved stopping that truck before it got off I-95. He couldn't think about the bad outcomes. He gripped the wheel hard. Leia was alive and he'd do everything he could to get her out of that container.

"Call Brunswick Police Department," he asked the car's hands-free system.

"Brunswick PD, is this an emergency?"

"Good evening, ma'am." Eric laid on a thick Georgia twang. "There's a pair of idiots on highway 17 racing, heading for I-95. Gotta be doing a hundred."

"Description of the cars, sir?"

"A black European sports car, a real fancy one. That son of a bitch almost killed me. That boy is driving that roller-skate like he stole it. The other idiot is in a big ass black Range Rover, and he keeps trying to force the other one into a ditch. They're getting on I-95 south. If they keep it up, it'll be one heck of a wreck."

He clicked off the call. Hopefully that would get the attention of some local LEO with nothing better to do tonight than help him rescue Leia.

ERIC JOINED the steady flow of southbound traffic and wove from lane to lane carefully, following Oblonsky and Larry, but not getting too close. He needed a plan. It was an hour drive to Jacksonville, Florida.

The loud ring of his cell in the car made him jump. He clicked the answer button on the steering wheel.

"Agent Simms, what does the federal government have for me?" He kept his eyes on the Rover ahead of him. The cynical part of him was ready to be disappointed.

"I have a highway patrol officer who's between you and the Florida border. He has some kind of plan. He was already working on intercepting a stolen A8. I assume that's you?"

Eric ignored the comment about the stolen car.

"One officer?" One highway patrol officer. That was a small step above a rent-a-cop. His call to Brunswick PD had gotten some attention. He just wished it had been more.

"Yes, but the locals are on their way from both Florida and Georgia to assist."

Eric felt a small trickle of hope. Enough law enforcement in one place and they would have to stop Oblonsky.

"Be sure they send medical response. If there are women in that container, they could be in bad shape." Images of the many ways Leia could be injured flashed across his mind. The thought was physically painful to him. He shook it off and refocused on driving.

"FBI tech is tracking your cell, so we have an exact location for you. Can you tell me about the semi we need to stop?" Simms was all business.

"Newer white Peterbilt cab and red shipping container. The Range Rover is all black with orange running lights on the front and sides."

Eric could hear Simms relaying the details to someone on another phone line in the background.

"Robb, you should be getting close to the roadblock now," Simms said a few minutes later.

He made a few strategic lane changes to get much closer to Oblonsky. He read the plate number off to Simms, who again repeated it to a third party.

Red brake lights flared all around him. He slowed and

rolled almost to a stop on the top of a small rise in a section of I-95 where the six lanes were divided by concrete K-rail and the right-side shoulder was narrow because of a steep slope down to an access road.

A single Georgia Highway Patrol car sat on the shoulder with lights flashing. A massive paving machine blocked the right lane of I-95, and a crew of construction guys were setting up cones and flashing signs indicating the need to merge.

The left lane had a disabled semi angled so it blocked the road and the center shoulder. The driver had wedged his truck up against the highway divider. The scene was staged perfectly, with orange safety triangles behind the stranded vehicle helping with authenticity.

Eric had to give the highway patrol officer credit. For one guy with no time to plan, he had a very effective road-block in place. The officer was slowing traffic to a crawl, waving cars through one at a time.

Eric drummed his fingers on the steering wheel as the line of backed up traffic inched toward the bottleneck. He was two cars behind Oblonsky.

"Simms, what's the plan?" Eric hated the anxiety in his voice.

"I can't tell you. Officer Jackson King on the ground is in charge, and I have no direct communication with him."

Eric hated getting second-hand information. He was flying blind, relying on an unknown highway patrol officer in nowhere, Georgia, to orchestrate Leia's salvation. His jaw ached from the tension of grinding his teeth.

"I think our truck driver is getting antsy. He's on and off the brakes and keeps weaving from side to side," Eric said. "I think Larry is going to do something stupid."

Larry was the weak link. Eric had already proven that

by getting him to talk after picking him up at the gas station. He had a bad feeling about this.

A line of Florida police vehicles with lights and sirens blazing came screaming up the northbound side of the highway. The caravan squealed to a stop just past Eric and used a break in the K-rail to U-turn before charging back south. Eric could feel the R8 sway when one of the Florida police SUVs whipped past him on the shoulder.

The officers swarmed out of their vehicles, setting up an impressive display around Officer King's roadblock. The Florida law enforcement response was breathtaking.

The show of force was also scaring the shit out of Larry.

The white Peterbilt shifted into gear and started toward the right shoulder, picking up speed as it went off the road. There was a small access road alongside the highway that led to a long stretch of country road. That had to be where Larry was going, but the semi was never going to make it down the incline.

Eric watched the truck, unable to do anything to stop it. The semi was sliding down the steep embankment, the cab and trailer both leaning. Soon physics would take over, and they would tip. He broke into a cold sweat. He was powerless. He gripped the wheel and waited for Oblonsky's reaction.

"Fuck, Simms, this is going to hell," Eric growled. He hammered the accelerator to chase after the Range Rover. It had left its lane and was following the semi toward the shoulder.

NINETEEN

LEIA GASPED. The truck was tipping, sliding, and suddenly she was too. The right side of the container dipped down. She slid across the metal floor, her pants snagging on the rough surface. She hit the far wall hard and bounced off into another woman. Their limbs tangled as they struggled for handholds. She felt her elbow slam into the woman's body.

The truck's brakes roared, and the sound of twisting metal was loud enough to drown out the women's screams. The container slid on its side, picking up speed. She tried to cling to the sidewall and frantically searched for a handhold. The LED lights were thrown around the box, lighting up the chaos like a strobe in a discotheque.

A deafening crash and enormous shudder rocked the container. Leia and the other women bounced off each other and the container walls like ragdolls. Pain vibrated through her brain when her head smacked hard against the metal wall. Finally, it slammed to a stop, tilted on its side. Leia fought to stay conscious. Her vision narrowed, eyes slipping closed. It would be so easy to let go and slide into the darkness.

The soft crying of the other captives penetrated Leia's fog. She touched the side of her head, and her fingers came away slick with blood. A woman half on top of her was trying to sit up. They twisted toward one another, wrapping their arms together, and helped each other sit up, resting their backs on what had been the container's roof.

The women were speaking to each other, but she couldn't understand what they were saying. Still woozy from hard hit to her head she could only watch as they helped each other sit up, evaluate injuries, and search for the LED lights that had broken loose in the crash. The idea of being trapped in this metal box without lights sent a shiver up Leia's spine.

"Leia? Are you okay?" Anna asked. She was the one who had untied Leia and was the only captive who spoke English.

"Yes, I think so. My head—"

Her reply was cut off by the distinctive ping of a bullet ricocheting off the outside of the container. The women let out panicked cries and held tight to each other. More shots, the ping, ping, ping coming fast one after the other. When the shooting stopped, Leia crumpled back against the cold metal wall, her chest rising and falling fast.

A groan from the rear door latch of the container sent a new wave of fear through the captives. The women huddled together, waiting for the door to open.

"Leia? Leia! Can you hear me?"

Leia struggled to her feet, stumbling over the others. "Eric!"

A sob of relief ripped out of her as she made her way to the door. She tumbled out and into Eric's waiting arms. He pulled her tight against his body and backed away from the listing cargo container. Carrying Leia, Eric stumbled over to sit with his back against a retaining wall.

Eric held her like she would shatter. His hands skimmed over her, stopping at her visible injuries. He pressed his lips to her hairline and whispered her name over and over. Leia let her tears flow, overwhelmed with relief.

She sat back so she could see Eric's face. A fine powder coated his skin, the kind from an airbag deployment. She brushed shards of safety glass off his shirt and out of his hair. His left shirt sleeve was sticky, and she was disturbed to see a bloody scrap of orange cloth bandaged his hand.

"Eric, your hand."

"It's nothing," he murmured.

He took his hand back from her and wrapped his arms around her before leaning forward to place the softest of kisses on her lips. "My hand isn't important. You're safe. That's what matters."

He tucked Leia's head under his chin, and she relaxed into his embrace, her eyes closed. Eric held her close, and she ignored the chaos around them. Her breathing relaxed, and her heart stopped racing. She was safe.

"I'm just a driver, you know, man. How the fuck would I know there were girls in the back?" Larry's voice cut through the rest of the noise at the scene, drawing Leia's attention. A uniformed officer pulled a handcuffed Larry up the embankment, ignoring his continued ranting.

She turned to watch paramedics help the last of the dazed captives from the container. They were huddled together on the access road at the bottom of the incline. The red light from the ambulances highlighted their wary faces and battered bodies. They were so young.

Beyond the container was the cab of the semi. The hitch had failed when the truck began to roll. The cab looked like a crumpled ball of tin foil. It must have rolled over several times. That Larry walked away was astonishing. She recalled Eric's comment that guys like Larry are human cockroaches, harder to kill than you think. It looked like he was right.

Eric had also been watching Larry's perp walk. "Poor Larry. He just doesn't know when to shut up," he said.

She glanced at Eric's face, and when their gazes met, they both started laughing. At first, it was just a small giggle from Leia, but soon they were gripping each other as a wave of almost hysterical laughter enveloped them.

Leia continued to chuckle, wiping away the happy tears that rolled down her face. Laughter was the best medicine. She could hardly feel her battered ribs, split lip, or bruised skull. She would heal, and so would Eric.

"Thank you for coming for me," she whispered into his ear, relaxing for what felt like the first time since she took Sal's files.

"Always."

A CHORUS of angry women's voices, shouting in Russian, erupted near the ambulances. Eric twisted with Leia still in his lap, looking for the source of the commotion.

Oblonsky, his shirt cut open and bloody bandages over his shoulder wound, was strapped to a stretcher that two paramedics pulled toward an ambulance.

"Bastard!" one woman screamed and lunged at him, her hands like claws. A medic pulled her back.

The vengeful women turned toward their captor, shouting in Russian, each trying to attack the injured Oblonsky. A few police officers joined the fray and gained control of the situation quickly, pushing the stretcher into a waiting ambulance that sped off as soon as the doors closed. Eric was reassured to see the women's response. They still had the will to fight; they weren't completely broken.

Leia gasped, and Eric followed her gaze to the wrecked Range Rover.

It lay in a twisted heap on the side of the steep slope just above the container with what was left of the Audi crumpled underneath.

"Were you in that car?" she asked.

"Yes," Eric admitted cautiously.

"What happened?" Her fingers curled tightly around his arm, the grip almost painful.

"Later." Eric pulled her in for another gentle kiss. The details could wait until she was cleaned up, rested, and had a glass of wine.

The kiss was a soft brush of the lips as he tasted her. Leia moaned quietly into his mouth and returned his kiss gently, slowly, like they had all the time in the world to enjoy each other. He savored the feel of her in his arms and angled his head to deepen the kiss for a brief moment before drawing back.

He resettled them against the retaining wall, stroking her hair, soaking up her presence. The frustration, anger, and fear that had been his constant companion since this morning when she never came back from the bathroom was finally gone. He leaned his head back on the cold hard wall. He was utterly thankful.

A few light raindrops floated down, landing on his face.

"Want to get out of here?" he asked Leia.

"Yes. A shower and food, then I want to sleep for a week."

"I have a plan." Eric pulled his cell out of his pocket

and exchanged a few texts. "Let's see if we can get out of here before the rain picks up."

Simms had said Officer Jackson King was in charge; Eric helped Leia stand and searched the scene for King. Near the wrecked semi cab stood a tall, good-looking man in his thirties. He wore a Georgia Highway Patrol uniform, including the trademark wide-brimmed hat, and was doing his best to bring order to the chaos. Eric and Leia hobbled up the incline. Between his bad knee and her multitude of injuries, they needed to help each other make the short walk.

"Officer King?" Eric asked when they reached him.

"It's Trooper, actually, but yes." The man had the demeanor and body language of an ex-soldier and a crisp voice without a trace of Georgia twang.

Eric introduced himself and Leia. He told King he was working with FBI Supervisory Special Agent Simms and that Leia's testimony would be instrumental in putting Oblonsky in jail. The trooper looked at Leia with appreciation.

"Any chance we can get out of here?" Eric asked, hoping the Simms connection would get them turned loose. The FBI had put King in charge of the scene until they had an agent on the ground.

"First, I need you to hand over the weapon used to shoot Oblonsky."

Eric glanced at Leia and shrugged. He was more than happy to admit he took a chance at ridding the world of the Russian scumbag.

"It's not my gun." He pulled the 9mm out and checked that there wasn't a bullet in the chamber before holding it out to Trooper King.

"Excuse me?" King produced a clear evidence bag and had Eric drop the firearm inside before sealing it.

"I was in a fight with a man I know as Max Davenport in Savannah today. It's his gun. I have no idea what you'll find when you run that weapon. Max isn't exactly an upstanding guy."

"Upstanding," Leia snorted. "That's an understatement. Max tried to kill us both in DC. Today he kidnapped me, offered to kill me for my old boss before giving me to Oblonsky."

"Okay, so not a good guy, got it." King looked down at the bagged gun. "Who is he?"

They both answered at the same time.

"My ex-partner," said Eric.

"Contract killer," said Leia.

King glanced between the two of them. "Does the FBI have all this information?"

"Yes, and we're happy to give them anything more they want," Leia said.

"We're both exhausted, dirty, and need food before we can help any investigation," Eric added, eyebrows raised, waiting for King to concede.

"Did the medics clear you guys?" King sounded skeptical. Eric was sure they looked like the walking dead.

"We'll be fine. I have a hard skull and can't wait to play doctor for Leia." He pulled her tight against his side before dropping a soft kiss on top of her head.

"I guess I can get someone to drive you to the cheap hotel at the next exit."

"I have a place for us to stay. We just need a ride," Eric countered.

Jackson waved to another trooper that was walking nearby. "Hey, rookie, take these two wherever they want to go. Bring back some coffee and doughnuts. Clean-up out here is going to take a while.

"One more thing, Robb. We're going to have to deal

with the grand theft auto issue at some point." Jackson waved at the destroyed R8.

"Just get me the owner's name and I'll buy the car from him. Full value, if he doesn't call the insurance company." Eric had learned two truths as a fixer. One, money remedies almost everything, and two, always leave the insurance company out of it.

"You know what one of those things cost?" Jackson looked incredulous.

"Yep." Eric gestured for the rookie to lead the way to his car.

"Where are we heading, sir?" the rookie asked Eric.

"The Inn at Samuel Hyde Island."

"Nice," the young officer replied.

TWENTY

INSIDE THE BATHROOM of the incredible cottage Eric had secured for them, Leia shrugged out of her clothes, peeling off the destroyed stuff like sloughing off an old skin. It felt so good to get rid of the dirty outfit. She examined her body in the gilded mirror. Scrapes and bruises marked her skin. Thankfully most looked like they would heal quickly. Her scabbed-over split lip from Sal's backhand even looked okay, but her wrists were a disaster from the cruel bite of the zip ties.

Before she turned the shower on, she heard bits and pieces a muffled conversation between Eric and the bellman who'd shown them to the cottage. They were talking while the young man built a fire for them in the bedroom's wood-burning fireplace. Eric was getting food and clothes delivered for them, despite the late hour.

A resort as exclusive as the Inn at Samuel Hyde Island must not get many guests checking in well after midnight without bags. Eric told the front desk employee that they had been in a car accident to explain their bedraggled state and arrival via police car. The alias he gave corresponded to a reservation for a beautiful private guest cottage on the property. Once the staff member saw that they were staying in one of the resort's most expensive rooms, she started oozing southern hospitality.

During the rainy golf cart ride from the main resort, the bellman told them their cottage had been built in 1892 for a famous oil tycoon as a winter vacation home. The main hotel building was the original hunt club, which was converted to an exclusive five-star beach resort a few decades ago when investors bought the Island. As they whipped along the cart path, Leia admired the Gilded Age architecture. The buildings were like wedding cakes with fancy stucco and lacey wood details. Dramatic nighttime lighting highlighted each building's best features.

Leia gingerly stepped into the hot shower, letting the strong spray rinse the dirt and dry blood off her skin. The bathroom may have been in a historic building, but it was the pinnacle of twenty-first-century plumbing. The glass and marble shower had more heads than she could count. She sucked her breath in through her teeth at the sting of the water on her open cuts.

"Are you okay?" Eric asked as he slipped into the bathroom, his expression concerned.

"It stings, but it's worth it to be clean."

"Let me help." He shed his clothing and stepped into the massive shower behind her. He took the washcloth and soap from her, and with infinitely gentle hands washed her battered body. Each wound he found seemed to cause him fresh pain.

Tipping her head back against his firm chest, he rinsed her hair before using shampoo to remove every trace of blood from the cut on her scalp.

He investigated the knot. "It's not too bad. No stitches needed."

Leia took Eric's injured left hand in hers, inspecting the dozens of cuts and slices. He tugged his hand free and pulled her back flush against his front, enveloping her in his arms. They stood like that, cocooned in the warm spray of the shower. Leia loved how protected she felt pressed against his large body.

"I don't think I could survive seeing you hurt ever again. When I saw that container flip and slide off the road, I was devastated. What have you done to me, beautiful?" Eric nuzzled her neck.

"I don't know," Leia replied, turning around in his embrace to press a kiss over his heart.

She plucked the washcloth from his hand and took her turn, washing every inch of his abused body. He was a gorgeous man, and each injury was a testament to his desire to protect Leia with his life. She held back tears, overcome by his devotion.

Across his ribs and shoulder, she found shadows that by morning would become bruises from the car's seat belt. The damage to Eric's left hand looked even worse clean. It was like he'd lost a fight with a paper shredder. A few of the slices might have needed a stitch.

Eric flipped on the overhead rain showerheads, and hot water cascaded down. Leia groaned. It felt so good running over her shoulders. Eric, too was enjoying the pummeling, rolling his neck and murmuring something about whiplash.

"I think we might melt if we stay in longer," Eric said finally.

"It feels so good. I just wanted to wash away all of it. The desperation of the women, the evil of Sal and Oblonsky, and my fear." Leia tipped her head back, letting the rain shower pour over her one more time before twisting it off.

Eric stepped out first, drying off, then securing a towel around his slim hips, leaving his muscled chest bare. He turned, holding out a second towel for Leia. She stepped out, and he wrapped her in the soft terrycloth.

He gestured at a robe on the hook. "Come on out when you're ready."

THE FIRELIGHT FLICKERED on the dull blue-gray walls and white wainscoting; the bedroom suite's herringbone brick fireplace faced a seating area nestled in a curved bay window. Eric, in a robe matching hers, was setting out a spread of cocktails, appetizers, and first aid supplies on the low coffee table in front of the overstuffed sofa in the bay window.

"What is all this?" Leia asked, taking a seat next to Eric.

"I think it was a wedding reception."

"What?"

"The inn is famous for destination weddings. Families book the cottages for accommodations and then the grounds, beach, or small chapel are the location for the ceremony. In the daylight, you'll see why. The island is spectacular."

"Okay?" She still didn't understand.

"The food and drinks I think were excess from someone's happy occasion." He passed her a plate filled with delicate hors d'oeuvres, each one prettier and tastier than the next.

She popped a smoked salmon something in her mouth and groaned in happiness. Eric pressed a martini glass into her hand and then, with a silly flourish, poured a pale pink concoction from a cocktail shaker for her.

She was about to take a sip when he interrupted her by rushing to plop in a garnish of berries and rosemary.

"Ta-da! The *Happily Ever After*." Eric held up a card with the cocktail recipe on it. She took the recipe card and saw that, on the bottom of the paper, it said *Ted and Robbin forever* in script.

"Yummy!" Leia decided Ted and Robbin were her kind of newlyweds. The drink was spectacular. A few more of these and she might feel almost human.

For a while, they ate in silence, picking out the best morsels from the tray of appetizers. Eric refilled both their glasses a few times. She welcomed the soft glow from the pink cocktail; it was better than a bottle of aspirin.

Breaking the silence, she asked, "You knew I was in the container? You shot Oblonsky? I'm so confused about what happened."

Eric recapped his day-long search for her and how he ended up in a stolen car chasing after her on I-95. Leia could tell he was trying to keep to the facts and not embroider the story to make himself a hero, but the truth was that he saved her.

She waited as he took another bite of food, chewing while he considered how to continue his story.

"Watching that semi roll over was horrific. As soon as the cab stopped rolling, Oblonsky's driver decided to make a break for the access road too, so I followed. The only way a little sports car was going to stop the Rover was a direct hit, so I waited until the SUV was off-balance, starting to nose down the steep embankment, and I gunned it, aiming for the Rover's high side, flipping it over. The Audi got tangled in the undercarriage of the Rover, and we rolled one on top of the other.

"I clawed my way out just in time to see Oblonsky fighting his way out of the wreckage, too. I knew he was going to run. I called out and told him to give up, but he turned and took a shot or two at me. I ducked behind what was left of the R8 and came up firing. I hit him in the shoulder and leg. It was the second time in my life I wanted to kill someone. I was so worried about what I would find when we opened the container."

Eric had saved her. He never gave up. She gave him a single hard kiss before returning to her spot on the couch. It seemed like everything was in place for the FBI to start making arrests. That was what she needed if she wanted to get her life back. She leaned back into the fluffy couch, head tipped back and eyes closed.

"No sleeping yet." Eric refilled her glass and then reached for the first aid supplies.

He expertly bandaged the worst of her injuries, a deep frown line appearing between his eyes while he worked. He spent the most time on her wrists, worried they might scar. The thought seemed to upset him more than it did her. She'd be fortunate if a few scars were the only permanent reminders of this ordeal.

Leia took a turn as nurse working on his injuries. She left his hand for last, not confident she could do much for it. He passed her a small tube of superglue, and instructed her to seal the cleaned out slices on his hand with it.

"Superglue? Is that a good idea?" she asked as she did it anyway.

He clenched his jaw against the burn from the glue when she sealed a particularly long gash that the razor wire had caused.

"It works in a pinch. Better than trying to sew myself up."

"You've done this before?"

"Never with such a lovely nurse assisting."

TWENTY-ONE

"CAN WE JUST RELAX, cuddle for a bit? My mind is still going a thousand miles an hour," Leia asked Eric.

"Not a problem." Eric tucked her back against his chest as they reclined on the plush couch.

"Watching the fireplace, hearing the flames crackle, it's nice. I need a little nice before I try and sleep. Although if this doesn't work, I can try a few more of those *Happily Ever Afters.*"

Eric chuckled. "They're pink, but they are powerful."

"I just keep second-guessing everything that happened, you know. What if I hadn't gone to the bathroom, what if we hadn't gone to the stupid bank?"

"The bank?" Eric asked, confused.

"Yeah, Sal said they found us from the security tapes at Mid City Bank."

Eric whispered an expletive and shook his head. "I can't believe that was our mistake. How many hours of security footage were they looking at to get lucky and find you? I had wondered if it was the rental of the carriage house. Either way, your boss was using every resource at his disposal to find you." Eric couldn't believe the lengths Sal gone to looking for Leia.

Leia relaxed back into his embrace. She ducked her head to give his right hand a quick kiss where it rested over her chest before falling silent. It was a good thing his connection to the island was secret; they would be safe here.

Eric relaxed into the cushions the crackling and heat from the fireplace was hypnotic.

He could feel her relaxing, the food and drinks dulling their aches and pains. The inviting bed was close, but Eric agreed they needed something to help work the adrenaline out and ease their minds before trying to sleep, and he knew the perfect remedy.

He let his hands wander, slipping inside the V in the front of Leia's robe. He found her nipples and caressed them, alternating between soft tugs and palming her whole breast. She pressed into his hand, arching her spine, her hips shifting back into his growing erection.

Her soft sounds and urgent cries chased away any lingering fear that he'd lost her. She was his again. Safe and whole, trusting him with her body. He needed this connection.

He pulled her robe open, exposing her torso. In the dappled firelight, her skin glowed, the bruises hardly noticeable. He skimmed his hands down her torso all the way to the warmth between her thighs. As he teased her slick flesh, she moaned, spreading her legs so he could touch every bit of her.

Her breath quickened, soft, low moans coming fast. Her eyes closed; she was close. He enjoyed every gasp.

He focused on the bundle of nerves nestled between her folds, stroking it with firm fingers. Her hips followed his rhythm, and he rubbed his hard cock against her beautiful ass. He pinched down gently with his finger and thumb. She trembled, moaning his name as she shattered.

He sat up halfway, straining to reach the condoms that were included with the first aid kit. The bellman had earned an extra tip for his attention to detail. When he finally managed to pluck a foil packet off the coffee table in front them, he tore it open, spread his robe, and covered his straining cock.

Relaxing back into place behind Leia, he pushed her robe up and then slid his cock between her thighs. Adjusting her hips with his hand, he entered her wet heat. He moaned into her ear, his lips trailing along her jawline.

She spread her legs and hooked one back around his thigh, her heel digging into his ass, helping him slide even deeper. She felt so good, the connection was unlike anything he'd felt before.

"Touch yourself for me. Come on my cock." He looked over her shoulder and down the length of her body to watch her hand dip below her stomach to find her clit. Watching her touch herself was beyond hot.

He began to thrust, short slow strokes that teased them both. Her relentless fingers were busy pushing her body toward a second climax. Her chest heaved with every breath, every moan, and her head rolled on his shoulder. She twisted her hips, her inner walls clamping down on his hardness as she chased her release.

She began to shudder around him, and he let himself go, speeding up his thrusts to match her grinding hips. They were both panting, mumbling each other's names. She cried out her release, and it sent him falling over his own edge. The waves of his orgasm rippled down his spine, he clenched his jaw and felt his cock jerk as he came.

He stayed buried inside her, pulling her tight to his chest. His lips found the shell of her ear and he nibbled softly on the tender skin. She was totally relaxed in his arms. Her trust was humbling, their intimacy totally fulfilling.

Contentment unfurled inside him; this was what he'd needed. Leia was in his arms and now he could relax. Her safety and happiness were all that mattered.

It was overwhelming to realize that what had started from a single phone call was turning into something so important. His heart thumped hard in his chest, his arms tightened around her.

She wasn't a client or a way to assuage his guilt for his past. She was the woman that he'd fallen in love with.

Reluctantly he rose from the sofa and walked to the bathroom. He stopped and looked back at her. She was so beautiful that it made him ache to leave her even for a moment. He brought back a damp cloth and helped her clean up.

"You ready for bed?" he asked.

She stretched, her robe still open, his eyes caressed her body. She mumbled her agreement, half asleep already.

Eric helped her from the couch, and together they found their way to the bed. Naked, they slipped under the crisp sheets, the embers of the fire still flickering. He fell asleep with her head on his chest, her hair tickling his nose.

She is my future.

"MY FATHER HAD me up at five every morning, starting in elementary school. I had chores and exercises, you name it. He was raising me to be a carbon copy of himself." Eric held a wine glass in one hand and an empty oyster shell in the other, gesturing with it as he spoke. The blue polo shirt strained over his well-developed chest. The hotel's logo was embroidered on the shirt over his heart; the preppy look wasn't the style she'd grown to expect from him. But when much of your wardrobe comes from the resort's gift shop, that happens.

"Then why didn't you end up in the military?" Leia knew his dad was a veteran.

They were sitting side by side, watching the sunset over Saint Simons Sound from a restaurant on the resort's pier.

"A question my father asks himself daily." Eric he smiled wryly and shrugged. "Simple answer, I don't take orders well. Longer answer, I think after all the years of dad's military discipline, I was ready to rebel. And there was my fascination with computers. I wasn't just writing code and playing video games but building systems from components I would buy online—total computer nerd."

"What? A computer nerd can't be a soldier?" She reached for another oyster from the ice-filled platter on their picnic table, adding a squeeze of lemon and a dot of cocktail sauce before tipping the slimy delicacy down her throat. The salty brine of the oyster was a perfect complement to the crisp March evening.

Leia took in the view, so different from the over-crowded waterways of New York. Here, the wide sand beaches had tree-sized driftwood bleached white by the salt and sun, and the Intracoastal waterway wound through tall marsh grass as far as you could see.

"I had spent six years at MIT away from my dad's pro-military views, and the killing of Osama bin Laden had just happened. It looked like the war on terror was winding down. I thought the FBI would be perfect for my skills. With dad's military instruction and my master's degree, I thought I would get into Quantico and whiz through training to become a field agent." He shrugged and stared off at the distant causeway bridge. "My bad knee put an end to any FBI dreams I had."

The waitress stopped at their table, refilling glasses with a golden Sauvignon Blanc, and taking an order from Eric for more oysters and some shrimp to share.

They had explored Samuel Hyde Island on foot and by beach cruiser bicycle. The island was beyond charming. The locally owned businesses had just opened up for the spring season and were thrilled to help two stranded travelers refill their wardrobes and stomachs.

When they weren't playing tourist, they explored each other's bodies. She hummed with arousal every time Eric touched her, but the connection they shared was more than sex.

Leia nudged him with her elbow, and he turned and gave her a quick peck on the cheek.

The last two days were like a little vacation. They had settled into an unspoken agreement where they didn't talk about the upcoming FBI investigation or any trial that might result. Leia had reveled in their time together. Like the date night in Savannah, these two days had been a tempting glimpse of what a long-term relationship with him might be like. What a normal life with him could feel like. And it was addictive.

Eric was her opposite in so many ways—brave when she was timid, bold when she was reserved. She wanted to plan every detail; he jumped in with both feet and let an adventure unfurl. They fit together in the most unexpectedly perfect way. He was larger than life with looks that turned heads. In the last two days, Leia had gotten used to receiving jealous stares when other women realized he was with her.

Unfortunately, she knew that the idyllic time was coming to an end. They'd go back to Savannah to meet with Agent Simms in the morning. Protected by the bubble of this island, Leia could see a future for them. But she wasn't sure if, just over the bridge, real life waited to destroy her illusion.

The beautiful sunset before them was happening over the very marsh Eric had raced the R8 across when chasing Oblonsky and Larry. The sun was just starting to dip low on the horizon, and in the distance, a container ship passed below the Brunswick causeway bridge heading for the port.

She tried to suppress a shiver. Could there be another container of women on that ship? Eric felt her tremble and was quick to offer his jacket, lifting it off the bench and standing up to place it around her shoulders.

"You okay? Too cold?" he asked, concerned.

"No, just missing this already." She leaned back, resting against his solid body. He put his hands on her shoulders and leaned down to steal an upside-down kiss. Tonight was perfect, a glimpse at the future she desperately wanted.

"HOW DID you know about this resort?" she asked when he sat back down. Their bubble wouldn't last much longer, and Leia was determined to enjoy every moment.

"Funny story. A few years ago, a client needed help disappearing for a little while…" He launched into a wild story about an exceedingly wealthy client who bought part of the resort after his stay. She let him talk, egging him on with nods and smiles, enjoying a carefree evening, making it count.

Here on this island she could acknowledge that she was in love with him. It was as easy as taking her next breath. Her heart was overflowing with emotions that she didn't even have names for, it was perfect.

But envisioning how this relationship looked back in

New York wasn't as easy. She was a jobless FBI witness. The investigation and trial were going to consume her life.

Giving up Eric wasn't an option she wanted to accept. She would fight but she was afraid that might not be enough. She wished they could stay on this island forever.

TWENTY-TWO

LEIA SHIFTED in the hard plastic chair. Agent Simms and Eric had left a little while ago to work through some logistical issues while she waited for another interview that was to start in a few minutes.

Simms had greeted them as soon as they arrived at the Savannah field office that morning. He'd gotten them coffee before going over Tuesday's events in detail. His respectful demeanor at first took Leia by surprise. It was a massive departure from his attitude when they met in DC last week. Today, it felt like the agent, and everyone she met with at the FBI, was on her side.

The door to the conference room opened, and a tall, athletic-looking woman in her forties entered. The woman had a short bob haircut with gray streaks and minimal makeup; she looked all business.

The woman extended her hand. "Miss Stone? I'm Janet Heinz. I work at the US Marshals office, as a Witness Inspector for WITSEC."

"Nice to meet you." Leia took the woman's hand, unsure what exactly this interview would entail.

"Simms asked me to speak with you to see if a future placement in the witness protection program would be right for you." The inspector took a seat, her expression serious but sympathetic. "You are a unique individual. What you did was very brave, and unlike ninety-five percent of the witnesses in our program, you aren't making a deal to avoid jail time."

Leia nodded, accepting the praise for her actions.

"Your decision to join WITSEC would be voluntary. We would offer you a new life, but at the expense of leaving this one behind. This is an important decision, not one to make lightly. Our program has a flawless success rate for witnesses that follow the guidelines."

"What exactly does that mean?" She wanted the unvarnished facts, not the sales pitch.

"No witness has ever been killed while in the program if they followed the rules. And there are several rules we would need you to follow to stay safe."

"What kind of rules?"

"We craft a new identity for you and will relocate you to a new city of our choosing. You'll give up your past. Name, job, education, everything will be new. An Inspector like myself and a small number of US Marshals would be the only people with knowledge of your past and your new identity. Keeping the information limited to very few people keeps you safe."

Leia's stomach turned. This was a life-altering decision. Could she give up everything she knew as Leia Stone and become someone else?

"Could I still work as a CPA?" Her career was her identity. Her education was one of her proudest accomplishments.

"It would be up to your Inspector to make the ultimate decision, but I would think not. Your past, including education and professional qualifications, wouldn't be part of your new identity."

Ms. Heinz pulled out a few forms from her satchel and placed them in the center of the table with a pen on top. "These are some basic personal information forms, a way for us to start crafting a new identity for you."

Leia pulled over the sheets. Just three pages. The opening questions were basic demographic ones. Below those, it asked her to list her friends and family. She paused. This was the list of people she would never communicate with again. Her heart thumped in her chest, and the pen wavered in her hand. The next question wanted a list of all the places she'd lived and visited often. Places she would never see again. She set the pen down.

Giving up every friend from high school and college and leaving New York, the city she loved, would be difficult. But abandoning the education she worked so hard for and never again being able to visit her parents' graves would shatter her. And any future she'd imagined with Eric would be impossible if she entered WITSEC.

"I want to talk this over with some people before I go farther," Leia said.

"That isn't recommended. Secrecy is safety." Heinz's eyes were deadly serious.

"I need time. You said this is an offer, not a requirement. I need to think. Talk with Simms." She was steadfast. This wasn't a choice she would rush.

"Are you considering including Eric Robb in the decision?" She didn't wait for Leia to answer. "I wouldn't recommend that. The man is barely better than the criminals you're working to put away."

Leia bristled at the unfair characterization.

Heinz reached under the table and pulled a thick paper

file from her bag. The file folder had the FBI emblem on the outside, and the tab had Eric's name on it.

"A man does not have an FBI file this size if he's a good person." She slid the large file toward Leia. "Take a look. I want you to see it in black and white."

Heinz pulled out her cell phone, dropping her eyes to the screen, giving Leia a semblance of privacy in which to read the file.

Leia sat back, leaning away from the file. She tamped down the unpleasant feeling that she was violating Eric's trust. Thinking about opening the file felt like reading someone's private diary—it felt wrong. He told her he wasn't a criminal, but the existence of this file seemed to indicate otherwise.

Exhaling, Leia decided that more information, more data was always best. She reached for the file cautiously like it might bite.

The newest reports were on top. A statement from Larry was first. Leia flipped past it without pausing. The next few documents were also about this week's events, the stolen car, security logs from the port. Scanning, she didn't see much.

Deeper in the file were documents regarding open cases where Eric was either the prime suspect or an accessory. All were recent, the last few years. The crimes were related to his work. Incriminating words jumped off the page at her: wanted for questioning, helped flee the jurisdiction, security breach, confidential information, wire fraud, intimidation, blackmail, destroying evidence, computer hacking, insurance fraud.

In many of the open cases, Eric was an accessory after the fact. He'd helped cover up a crime or enabled the individual that was the primary focus of the case to avoid prosecution. Money, so much money, was involved in every case. The sums were staggering. The other parties involved were high profile—politicians, actors, and business people.

The accusations seemed creditable but a far cry from the human trafficking and drug dealing of Sal and his clients. Eric said he bent the rules. Reading this, Leia felt like he had twisted them into pretzels. His actions were outside the letter of the law, but she'd expected that. Rather than make her uncomfortable, Eric's file reaffirmed what she already thought.

She flipped to a new report. It was the first time she saw Max Davenport's name in the file. This report was old, not in sequential order like the rest of the documents. It was an open homicide case, murder for hire, and so were the next four. Leia thought of Max proposing to dump her body in the marshes. She knew he was a killer. The reports were incomplete, missing key facts, and heavily redacted. Their inclusion suggested that Eric was involved in the plots, but the evidence wasn't there. Leia knew in her heart it was because Eric wasn't part of Max's crimes.

The next section was cases like the current ones open against Eric, but they involved Max as well. She flipped through these older cases quickly when she realized they were no different than the current ones—a lot of rule-bending, very little violence.

Only three things remained in the file: two slim stapled packets and a loose sheet of paper. The first packet was Eric's application and rejection from the FBI training program. Leia skimmed it; the notes matched what he'd told her. No law enforcement training and pre-existing injury.

The second packet was thicker; it was Max Davenport's FBI application and rejection. Reading the psych evaluation, Leia felt the hair on the back of her neck stand: *Davenport's psychological testing fits the classic picture of psychopa-*

thy, but he was able to avoid early contact with the judicial system because of parental oversight and enlistment in the Army. His dishonorable discharge and other antisocial behavioral tendencies render him unfit for consideration to become an agent. Retain file for reference in case of future instability or violence against the Bureau.

Leia could easily accept the finding that Max was a psychopath.

The final item was a photocopy of a handwritten paramedic's report from five years ago.

The patient was a white male, only identified by the first name *"Max."* A 9-1-1 call from a neighbor reported a disturbance, leading to his discovery. The apartment address didn't mean anything to Leia. The patient was unresponsive when found; he presented with hypoxia and signs of strangulation. The medic established an airway, began CPR, and successfully restarted the patient's heart with a defibrillator.

Leia reread the paramedic's report. This was the explanation for Max's survival. Leia glanced up. Heinz was still looking at her cell. Leia quickly slid the single sheet of paper out of the folder and folded it into quarters before stuffing it in her pocket. Eric deserved to see the report.

She closed the folder and slid it back to Heinz.

"I'm sure you can see that a man like that could be a huge risk to your safety if you're in the program." Heinz reclaimed the folder and tucked it away.

"Eric would never put me or any client at risk. That file proves the lengths he's willing to go. Reading it doesn't change my opinion," Leia replied honestly. Her faith in Eric was growing stronger every day.

Heinz sighed like she was disappointed. "This isn't a decision you need to make today. They'll need you in New York for the grand jury hearings. It would be the time between indictment and trial when it would be most important for you to join the program. Depending on the outcome of the trials, it might eventually be safe for you to exit the WITSEC program."

Leia nodded, not knowing much about criminal proceedings. She had no idea what kind of time Heinz was talking about. She needed Google, or a lawyer to help explain all of this. It was overwhelming.

"I've been doing my job long enough to know that this is a hard decision to make, but I urge you to think seriously before you decline our help. The US Marshals are the best at this, and you have angered some powerful people. You need protection. The criminal trials could last a significant length of time."

Heinz's cell phone vibrated on the tabletop. She answered, agreeing with whoever was on the other line a few times before hanging up.

"Simms is ready for you, and we're done for now." Heinz held out her card for Leia to take. "Call me anytime. We can come for you."

TWENTY-THREE

ERIC ALWAYS CONSIDERED FLYING on a private plane a good thing: big comfortable chairs, no lines for luggage, and free drinks. Still, the return flight to New York was uncomfortably tense. Leia was quiet and looked overwhelmed, Simms was on the phone getting agents in New York ready to raid Sal's office, and Eric was at loose ends.

The support of the FBI relieved him of the burden of acting as Leia's sole protector. For the airport ride, the FBI arranged a full protective team. There was even clearance for the cars out onto the tarmac. Eric just followed along, useless as tits on a bull.

He switched seats, moving next to Leia, who had curled up in a ball under a fleece blanket. For the last twenty minutes, she'd been staring at the same spot on the floor.

"Hey, what's running through that brain of yours?" he asked.

"You were right. I'm not getting my old life back anytime soon, am I?" She was worrying the corner of the blanket, twisting it into loops around her fingers.

"No, beautiful, you're not. But the FBI is on board. They're pulling out all the stops to protect you. And prosecute the bad guys. You got everything you wanted. My job is done."

She should be relieved, but when he looked at her, she was tense. They believed her. And, based on the conversation Simms was having on his cell phone, the case against Sal was moving forward.

"It's overwhelming." Her voice sounded hollow, tired.

"You should listen to them. They know what they're doing." He reached out to cradle her face in his hand. She closed her eyes for a moment and turned her face into the caress.

"Okay, you're right." She sat up, dropping the blanket and finding her bag. She pulled a card out and passed it to Eric.

He looked down to read it: Janet Heinz, US Marshals Service, Federal Witness Protection Program. He hadn't expected this. The Feds were going to disappear Leia. He ran a hand down his face and gave Leia back the card. His stomach was in knots thinking about her in witness protection.

"She said I didn't have to decide about the program yet. She said after the grand jury."

"It would be safer than anything else." The truth tasted bitter on his tongue.

"I don't know…" Leia trailed off, her eyes searching Eric's face for some sign.

He wasn't sure what he could give her. Looking at her right now, he wanted to pull her into his arms and keep her with him. He couldn't rationally justify that. He got her what she wanted; the FBI was behind her. He should step back, let the Feds protect her. Make it easy for her to accept their help even if it felt like his chest was going to cave in.

The fact was the FBI could do more for her than he could. She didn't need him, the FBI had more man power and resources. Wanting to have a life with her because he loved her was one thing. But it was selfish to put her in danger to get what he wanted. Witness protection was a complication he'd never imagined. Her future with or without him was on an uncertain path.

He placed a kiss on her forehead, pausing to enjoy the smell of her hair. It felt a little like a goodbye.

"It will be good to go home to my apartment," she muttered when he pulled back.

"Yeah, it'll be nice."

Inside a voice screamed at him, telling him no, it wouldn't be good. Good was staying with Leia, but she hadn't invited him. It was time he faced the facts. He'd done his job. It was time to step back, even if it hurt. His chest ached, and he had to stop himself from rubbing at the pain.

WHEN THE PLANE landed at Teterboro Airport, a pair of FBI agents met them on the tarmac with a standard-issue black SUV. The agents, one blond and one Latino, looked younger than Eric. *This better not be her security detail.* Both were big, fit guys in dark suits with shoulder holsters, but they were closer to Leia's age than Eric was, making them nowhere near experienced enough in his opinion. Her boss was going to be looking for revenge, and they were back in Sal's home city.

"Look, Simms, are these two all you got?" Eric hooked a thumb over his shoulder at the two guys. He'd pulled

Simms aside out of Leia's hearing. The two young agents were transferring the luggage from the plane to the SUV.

"Those two are her personal protection detail. Both are ex-military and have excellent reputations in the Bureau. They've been with the New York field office for a few years. We also have eyes on her building and will be taking precautions when bringing her to the office," Simms replied. His tone was patient and professional.

Eric ran a nervous hand down his face; it wasn't enough.

"I can get some private security to back you up. Just give me a few hours. I can call in some favors." Eric was getting desperate. His voice was too loud, edging toward angry. Losing control of this situation was unacceptable. Leia was his responsibility, damn it. He reached for his cell, but Simms caught his hand before he could dial.

"Look, Eric, we have this. It's what we do. Thank you for taking care of our girl, but she's our responsibility now."

Eric stalked away from Simms before he threw a punch at the guy for doing his job.

The words *our girl* set his teeth on edge. She was his girl...wasn't she? Fuck, this was why he never did the relationship thing. He hated this feeling. The tangled-up sensation in his chest was getting worse. He didn't do hypotheticals, and relationships were built on those. And a relationship with someone who might end up in witness protection was worse than hypothetical—it was a mirage.

When he turned back to the SUV, everyone was already inside, waiting on him. He jogged over to the open backseat door and got in, immediately searching for Leia. He found her curled up in the third row alone. She looked small, huddled in the back. Eric wanted to wrap her in his arms and tell her whatever she needed to hear.

The trip into the city from New Jersey was quick for a weekday. Before Eric was ready to abandon Leia to the FBI, the SUV pulled to a stop in front of his Upper East Side apartment building.

Desperation. That's what he felt. He wanted her, but her future wasn't her own.

Eric reached over the seat. His fingers wrapped around her slender ankle. She looked up, startled from her trance, and their eyes met. She blinked hard, like she was fighting tears. He ran his thumb over her soft skin.

"I'll leave the burner cell on if you want to talk," he said.

He wanted to say more. Tell her he loved her. *But was that fair?* Or would it just add a new complication to her life when she was already grappling with a monumental decision. Besides, the backseat of an FBI SUV with three agents wasn't the place for a grand gesture.

He paused, every part of him hoping she would say something.

"Okay."

He nodded, acknowledging her quiet reply. He started to get out, his legs almost refused to obey.

"Wait," she said. She passed him a square of folded paper. "This should answer some questions."

Eric took the paper and got out of the car. A scrap of paper wasn't what he'd hoped for. He retrieved his bags from the back and met Simms on the sidewalk.

Eric shook the agent's hand. "Keep her safe for me." It physically hurt him to make the request.

"Will do." Simms's expression was sympathetic as he got back in the SUV.

Eric watched the vehicle pull into the city traffic, heading away from him and toward Brooklyn. He felt almost as helpless as he had in Brunswick when Oblonsky tossed her into that shipping container. She was only going to Brooklyn, he reminded himself.

He looked up at his building. It had to be safer than hers. It had cameras, a doorman, and all the security measures wealthy New Yorkers wanted. He could call Simms and convince him to turn around.

He took a deep breath of the New York City air, heavy with exhaust fumes. Fuck! He snatched up his bags and turned toward the entry to his building, nodding at the doorman who let him in and waved him toward the open elevator. His job was done.

Leia didn't need him. She had the Feds. It was safer for her this way.

He was a thirty-three-year-old man who had avoided meaningful relationships like the plague. Still, he'd managed to fall in love in just over a week with a do-gooder accountant who might disappear into the witness protection program without warning.

He dropped his bags and toed off his shoes in the entryway of his empty apartment. He needed a drink.

A tumbler of iced vodka in hand, Eric sat at his desk, the four computer monitors buzzing to life. He unfolded the paper that Leia had given him. It was a five-year-old paramedic's report detailing Max's resurrection. How the hell did she get it?

This paper was the scrap of evidence that might get him the answers he'd been asking about Max. He wasn't sleeping under the same roof as Leia tonight, but he would be working to find Max, one of the threats that could land her in the WITSEC program.

LEIA FUMBLED WITH HER KEYS, fitting them into the sticky lock on the outside of her building. When they arrived at the older brick midrise in Crown Heights, Simms had handed her the purse she'd left in the Savannah carriage house. She hadn't expected to see it again, but she was grateful to have her keys. Having to find her sketchy Super to let her into the apartment would've been just another complication.

When she gave Simms a strange look, he explained, "Eric and I ran a few errands today, tied up loose ends like your things and a borrowed Jaguar."

Leia led the agents up the three flights of stairs to her apartment. Breathing the familiar dusty smell of the old stairwell helped her relax. She was home. It had been less than two weeks.

Her place was a decent size for a single girl in New York, but the three big men standing in her living room seemed to take up every inch. The apartment had a definite feminine flair with simple light-colored furniture and dark green accents. The original dark parquet flooring, which had recently been refinished, glowed softly in the light of the setting sun coming in the windows.

Leia let out a big exhale and met Simms's gaze and waited for her next instructions. She was adrift, and he was all she had since Eric seemed to be taking a back seat to the FBI. Eric was her touchstone during the chaos of the last week, and without him, she was floundering. His words from the plane kept echoing in her mind. *My job is done.* What did that mean?

"I guess now is a good time to do formal introductions," Simms began, interrupting Leia's thoughts.

First, Leia focused on the tall blond man. Agent Wallace. He gave her hand a firm shake when introduced. He was a big guy, looked like a Viking. Blond hair a bit longer than she would think the FBI liked, and serious blue eyes. He could have been on the cover of a romance novel, just rip off his shirt and pass him a broadsword.

Next to him was Agent Reyes. He gave her a quick smile and a fist bump. She didn't know FBI agents gave fist bumps. The twenty-something guy gave off a vibe that made Leia think he would be the type to crack jokes and buy shots at the bar. His dark eyes sparkled with life, and when Simms explained the two men would both spend tonight at Leia's, he answered with a hearty *Hooah*. Must be ex-Army. That made her feel safer already.

"Monday will be soon enough for you to meet with our forensic accountants. For the weekend, Wallace and Reyes are going to split up guard duty. Learn your routine and help keep you out of danger," Simms explained for her benefit; the two agents seemed to already be in the loop.

"There is a local cop in a car on the street watching the building as well. I don't want you to feel like a prisoner in your apartment, but until we can get Sal Marino and the rest of his conspirators under arrest, I'd like you housebound." Simms was serious. There was no trace of the dismissive attitude he had for her safety when they met in DC.

Was it the evidence that got his attention or her kidnapping? After a quick conversation with Wallace and Reyes, Simms nodded goodbye to Leia from across the apartment before leaving.

Wallace pulled out his phone. "Leia, what's your favorite delivery around here? The FBI is buying dinner."

"Give me a second. I have a ton of menus." She went to the kitchen and found her stash.

When she saw the one for Fong's, she paused. She'd promised to introduce Eric to the best Chinese takeout in New York when they were in Savannah. She gathered the rest of the menus, leaving the one for Fong's in the drawer. She just couldn't stomach General Tso's chicken after that thought. She walked back to the waiting agents to look at the options.

She was pretty sure Reyes had eaten twenty pounds of Thai food before declaring himself finished. How the agent could stay looking like a fitness model when packing away that much food was a mystery. The guys were nice, a good distraction from her situation. They had kept up some mindless banter during dinner, occasionally drawing Leia in for a woman's perspective on their conversation.

Leia wanted to set Reyes up with the new intern at the office. They'd be a great match. She almost said so until she remembered that calling her former co-workers from Marino & Associates was probably not a good idea. Her new normal was looking like a lot of time spent with law enforcement until she got dumped wherever WITSEC wanted to abandon her.

"Here you go." Leia brought out a few blankets and some pillows and set them on the couch. "Sorry there's no second bedroom, but make yourselves at home. I'm going to head to bed." It had been a long day.

The agents had already flipped on March Madness basketball and were comparing brackets. They assured her they would both be there all night.

Alone in her bedroom, Leia's thoughts went to Eric and the future. They hadn't talked about a relationship, but she couldn't believe he'd vanish from her life now that they were in New York. His job was done, the phrase kept repeating in her mind, giving her a headache.

She wished she could talk to him, but the only way would be to borrow an agent's cell phone. That felt awkward. She didn't have a house phone. Glancing at her bed, she realized she was dreading sleeping without Eric tonight.

Leia reached for her bags; it was time to tackle unpacking.

The knapsack she'd left at the carriage house held everything she had brought from New York when she fled work last Wednesday. Wow. Only ten days ago, but it felt like a lifetime. She dumped the clothes all into a laundry basket to deal with later.

The two large canvas bags from the Samuel Hyde Island gift shop held all the clothes Eric had bought her over the weekend. He had more fun buying outfits for her than she did. Unexpectedly, he was something of a clothes horse. She should have guessed—the suit he wore to their first FBI meeting was exquisite, obviously tailormade for him.

The clothes themselves were unlike what she would have bought for herself. She stuck to traditional basics for work, and her casual clothes were pretty much what she wore in college. Eric had pulled out colors and cuts she would never have selected. The outfits were all so lovely, expensive, and beautiful. He'd managed to choose not only things she needed for the brief stay on the island but also modern work clothes that she knew looked a million times better than the boring basics she'd been buying for years.

Looking at the clothes, many still with tags, she felt like she should return them...or pay him back. Without a job, she wasn't sure how that would happen. She owed Eric so much, and not just money.

She started hanging up the clothes from the second bag when she found two items she didn't expect. A new phone and new tablet, both in gleaming white boxes ready to be opened. A sticky note on the outside of one said: "Sorry I nuked your old ones—Eric."

She plopped onto the edge of the bed, staring at the handwritten note.

Loving Eric could be frightening, but never seeing him again was even more devastating. The possibility that she would need to disappear was a roadblock on whatever path they might try to take. That was the problem—being ripped away from everything she knew by WITSEC would only be that much more traumatic if she and Eric were together. Ugh, her headache was back with a vengeance.

Leia unwrapped the new cell and plugged it in to charge. First thing in the morning, she would get the cell phone set up so she could call Eric. She wanted to talk with him, but not when Simms or any other FBI agent was listening.

If she didn't give this relationship a chance, she would hate herself. Every bad date, every stupid online dating profile, she would think of this night and regret having given up on what might have been.

After a hot shower, Leia donned her favorite silky PJs and climbed into bed and fell asleep. Alone.

TWENTY-FOUR

"HUSH, HUSH, PRETTY GIRL," Max hissed into Leia's hair. His right hand, still in a dirty cast held her wrists in a vice-like grip, and his massive body pinned her to the bed. "I can see why Eric wants you."

She bolted awake as adrenaline surged through her veins. She squirmed, desperate to dislodge the huge man, but she was trapped in the bed, helpless. She opened her mouth to scream.

"Don't bother. Your guards can't help you." Max dragged his scruffy face up the side of her neck, sniffing her hair and making Leia's skin crawl. "So sweet," he murmured, his lips caressing her cheek.

Leia felt the first tears run down her face; her loud sob echoed in the too-quiet apartment.

She bucked her hips, trying to get a leg free to kick at him with, but the tangled sheets held fast. Max shifted so he was next to her, his tree trunk sized thigh holding her to the mattress.

He raised his left arm above them, a glowing cell phone clasped in his fingers. He pointed the phone's front-facing camera at their heads sandwiched together on her pillow. On the screen, she saw a cruel parody of a couple's selfie lit by the camera's flash. Her tear-stained face filled most of the screen until Max adjusted the aim, filling half the frame with his head. His disheveled beard looked even more unkept in the harsh camera light, and the cut above his eyebrow was a jagged mess.

"Think Eric will like it?" The click of the camera shutter sounded, and Max dropped the phone.

He rolled back on top of her and bound her hands with zip ties. The stiff plastic ties cut into the bandages around her wrists. They were still raw from Savannah. She stifled the urge to fight the bonds. Her damaged skin was already screaming in pain from him restraining her with his hands.

Max rose, dragging Leia to her feet. Her mind flooded with images from the last time she was at his mercy. The airplane hangar, the drugs, being tossed into the container. Panic threatened to overtake her. Her breathing was erratic and darkness clouded the edges of her vision.

Her legs wouldn't support her. Max tugged her roughly to his side and half-carried, half-dragged her out of the bedroom, heading for her front door.

Glancing toward her small kitchen Leia could see the feet of one of her protection detail extending beyond the cabinets. She tried to go limp, make it harder for Max to pull her toward the door. She would be safer in her apartment. Max's steps never faltered. He crushed her against his side, squeezing the air from her lungs and lifting her feet off the ground. He trudged out the door and into the hallway.

"Don't think about screaming or calling for help. I will fucking kill you and anyone that interferes." He waved a gun under her nose. She stifled a sob.

Max shoved open the metal fire door that led to the stairs. Before he began to climb, he tossed Leia over his shoulder like she weighed nothing. He climbed the two flights of stairs, his shoulder digging into her soft belly. She hung her head, focused on the tread of the stairs. Step by step, she focused on getting herself together. After everything she'd survived in the last ten days she wouldn't give up when she finally had the FBI on her side.

At the top landing, he dumped her on the ground and kicked open the door to the roof. He caught the door with his foot and grabbed her bound hands, dragging her to her feet. Pain shot up Leia's arms. Her wrists were surely bleeding. She whimpered at the rough treatment, stumbling, the asphalt roof digging into her bare feet. Max tugged at her sore wrists, not slowing his steps.

On the roof, he pulled her to a low wall and pushed her down to sit on it. He grabbed her wrists and used another plastic tie to secure them to a U bolt that stuck out of the bricks between her legs. The cold wall and biting New York air cut through her thin silky pajamas. She shivered.

The cell phone was in Max's hand again. "Just sending Robb our picture."

He paced the length of the roof, back and forth, agitated. He dragged his hands through his hair and picked at the scab on his eyebrow with nervous fingers.

He stopped and turned to Leia, the light from the surrounding buildings was bright enough to illuminate his face. He was even more deranged looking than the last time she saw him. Eyes wide, teeth grinding. He knelt down to her level.

"You know he killed me once. Five years ago. I was dead, just for a few moments," he said, sounding like he was confiding a secret.

In the gloom, she could see sweat beading on his forehead while she tried to control her shivering. He returned to pacing, muttering to himself, his steps erratic and clumsy. He fumbled for his phone every few minutes, clicking buttons, like a teenager refreshing their social media feed.

It wasn't the same Max that breached her hotel room. In DC, he was a soldier. He had stealth and finesse and carried enough gear to outfit a SWAT team. Tonight, he looked like a mad man with a gun and a cell phone.

Leia clenched her jaw to still her chattering teeth. The wind was cold on the fifth-floor roof. Her bare feet felt like they should be blue.

"It was bad, so bad." He stopped walking to talk to her. "I visited hell, just for a few moments, but I am not going back." Shaking his head, he returned to his unpredictable pacing, again checking his cell—more muttering.

Max whipped around. "Why is Eric taking so long?"

Leia felt the anger rolling off him. It came on suddenly, no apparent trigger. In two steps, he was towering over her, a hand fisting her hair, tipping her head back as he demanded answers. "They want to know why he isn't here yet."

"Brooklyn...it's far," she told him through her shivers, not sure if they were from fear or cold. Her eyes watered from the painful yank of her hair.

"You're just bait." He released her, stepping away, apparently satisfied with her answer.

"Bait?" she squeaked. A new wave of fear engulfed Leia. What if Eric took the bait? He wouldn't abandon her. He would risk his life for hers. He wouldn't know that his death, not hers, was Max's goal. She should have fought harder when she was in the apartment, made a noise in the hallway, anything that would have kept her off this roof, and Eric safe from Max's trap.

"I need Eric. It's his blood that can pay my debt. Set me free." Max's cryptic reply multiplied her concerns.

Restrained and shivering, Leia had one weapon: her voice. She could feed Max's instability, push him from erratic to unhinged, use his psychosis. Give Eric an advantage.

"Why Eric?" she asked, her voice surprisingly steady.

"They want him, a trade, for my freedom." Max's voice wavered, his eyes darting around the roof.

"Freedom from what?"

"The demons that follow me, that talk to me, that find joy in blood and death." He gestured to the empty roof, pointing at his invisible tormentors. He rechecked his cell phone, shaking his head, angry what he wanted to see on the screen wasn't there.

What the fuck happened to this guy? Keeping him talking seemed like a good strategy. His movements were becoming more and more disjointed, and his voice louder.

"What demons?"

"I brought them back from hell. I am never alone." He turned and looked at Leia, anguish filling his eyes. "I just want to be alone."

STANDING on a side street in Crown Heights, Brooklyn, Eric pulled his black gear bag out of the trunk of his car. The older brick five-story building looked like many in the area. Halfway up the block, there was an unmarked car with a sleeping cop in it. So much for the FBI handling security. It looked like his job wasn't done.

On the drive across the city, he'd broken every traffic

law there was and almost forced a few cars into the East River. He focused on driving, trying not to think about Leia and the fear on her face in the cell photo. If Max had hurt her, he would kill him again.

He had two options for getting to the roof, inside stairs or an aging and rickety exterior fire escape. Speed or surprise. Shitty choices. Looking up to the roof, he swore he saw a glow of light for a moment, like a cell phone. Max.

He'd seen what Max could do to a defenseless woman. The needle poised above the arm of the Senator's twenty-two-year-old mistress flashed into his mind. Forget surprise. He needed to get up on that roof now. Running to the front of the building, he dropped his shoulder and slammed into the door. The old lock was a piece of junk and gave way under the assault.

He pounded his way up the stairs fueled by pure anger. He needed a clear head; it was time to get his emotions under control. He would save her. There was no alternative.

Breathing hard, he skidded to a stop at the roof access door. He could see the busted lock where Max had already forced it open. He slowed his harsh breathing and nudged the door open an inch, pressing his ear to the gap. He could hear Max. His tone was inconsistent, loud, then soft, ranting, then imploring. The words were indistinct. Eric was too far away to understand what he was saying.

He tilted his head, opening the door a bit more, peeking through the opening with one eye. Max wasn't visible, but Leia sat huddled on a low wall, her hands tied in front of her. She looked cold. Eric felt the tiniest amount of relief that she was alive and uninjured. It looked like she was talking to Max.

He let the door close softly. He pulled a tactical knife

out of his gear bag and strapped it on his belt. Double-checking his 9mm, he chambered a round before returning it to a shoulder holster and strapping a small revolver to his ankle. He was as ready as he could be, going in alone.

Max's text said no cops, no FBI, come alone, and Eric had followed his ex-partner's rules. But now it was time to call in the cavalry. He retrieved his cell from the gear bag and texted Simms: *Max has our girl on the roof. I am going to get her.*

He flipped the cell on silent and shoved it into his back pocket. He took a deep breath, calm and focused just like his father had drilled into him over decades of training. He boxed up his emotional turmoil, his fears, and his dreams. It was time to be a soldier.

He eased the door open and crept onto the gloomy roof. He stepped forward and turned until he could see Max, on the far side of the roof near Leia.

"Max?" he called. His put his hands out, palms facing forward. He didn't want to agitate him. Max already seemed to be at a breaking point. Gone was the military bearing. He was a dirty, disheveled husk of what he'd been five years ago. Hell, even a few days ago in Georgia, he'd looked more like himself, but now he was almost unrecognizable.

"Robb, nice of you to join us. Come over and say hello." Max stepped up behind Leia, his gun wavering in unsteady hands as he pressed it to her temple. "Far enough, stop."

Eric stopped. A small whimper of fear from Leia ripped at his heart. He needed her off the roof and safe so he could focus. She looked defenseless: bound, gun to her head, shivering in thin pajamas, her bare feet pale against the black rooftop.

Max bent down and ripped Leia's bound hands free

from the bolt in the wall. She moaned in pain and cradled her wrists to her chest. Max pulled her to her feet, pinning her against the length of his large body. They faced Eric across the roof.

"Remove your weapon and toss it back there." Max nodded toward the dark section of the roof behind him, where the building's mechanical equipment sat.

Eric complied, tossing the gun into the darkness. It clattered loudly.

Max shoved Leia at Eric. "Say your goodbyes. This is between us, partner."

Her bound hands trapped between them, Eric held Leia against his chest. He breathed in the familiar floral scent of her hair and rubbed his cheek against the soft strands. His hand cradled her head for a kiss.

Eric needed this kiss. The feel of her against him was the only thing that would stop him from telling her he loved her. He couldn't burden her with his declaration if he were fated to die tonight. He wanted her to remember this kiss but never feel remorse that loving her sent him to his death. A hundred times, he would choose to trade his life for hers.

She shivered in his arms. Her body was like ice. Her lips parted, and she leaned into the embrace, her need matching his. The kiss was too brief. He lifted his head and met her gaze.

"Eric, I need you to survive this." Her eyes sparkled with unshed tears as she flattened one of her bound hands over his heart.

He didn't trust himself to speak. He leaned his forehead against hers, closing his eyes for one heartbeat. He would do as she asked, he would find a way to survive or die trying.

He stepped back from her, pushing her toward the

stairway door. In a raspy, emotional voice he hardly recognized as his own, he told her, "Get somewhere safe."

LEIA STUMBLED through the door and sprinted down the stairs, her bound hands held to her chest. Her icy bare feet slapped against the cement, the sound filling up the empty stairwell. Her mind raced. She needed a plan and way to help Eric—a weapon or distraction.

She raced for her apartment door, fumbling with the doorknob, her wounded wrists oozing blood around the plastic ties. She stumbled inside, breathing hard.

Agent Reyes was in her kitchen, kneeling over Wallace's body, a cell phone pressed to his ear. Reyes's eyes lit up when he saw her. She stepped around the unconscious man to get a kitchen knife from the butcher block and passed it to him to slice her hands free.

"She's here," Reyes said into the phone before giving it to her.

"Hello?"

Agent Simms fired a series of questions at Leia about the situation on the roof. He was adamant that she stay in the apartment with Reyes. An FBI team with a sniper was en route. They would handle it.

After answering a few more of Simms's questions, Leia understood why Eric hadn't waited for the FBI to stop Max. Waiting was impossible. She had to act. She hung up on Simms, cutting him off.

Reyes was still checking out Wallace. The big man moaned and his eyelids shifted, but he remained out of it. Reyes pressed a kitchen towel to Wallace's head wound. Blood soaked the white cloth quickly.

"I'm going back up there, with or without you," Leia said.

"Leia, backup is coming. Just wait for them. You'll get yourself killed."

"I can't. I can't wait. You haven't seen Max Davenport, heard him talk. The man has lost touch with reality. All he wants is Eric dead." She swept up the kitchen knife and sat down to tug on an old pair of running shoes.

"A knife? You're going up there to stop a contract killer with a knife? Fuck." Reyes ran a hand over his face. "I can't convince you to wait for backup, can I?"

"No." She wouldn't stand down. Toe to toe with Reyes, she willed him to help her.

He looked at Wallace, still motionless on the kitchen floor.

"Tell me about the layout on the roof. Where are they standing? All the details you can."

Leia explained the situation. Reyes nodded, asking questions, looking for a tactical advantage.

"So if I come up the fire escape, the AC units will keep me hidden?"

"Yes, if Max is still standing where he was when I ran."

"Good. You promise to stay with Wallace?"

Leia nodded.

"Only open the door for the FBI or Paramedics," he said while checking his weapon.

Leia reached out, touching his arm. "Thank you."

He turned to head for the window in her bedroom and the fire escape. "Don't thank me yet."

TWENTY-FIVE

EXECUTED while kneeling on the roof of a Brooklyn apartment building wasn't how Eric imagined his death.

Researching the paramedic's report last night generated a single finding: the record of a non-voluntary psychiatric commitment. Just a week after his near-death experience, the hospital where Max was recovering transferred him to a mental hospital. The medical records painted a grim picture. He'd become violent with staff and suffered reoccurring delusions. A general diagnosis of psychosis had been rubber-stamped on the file.

Watching Max, Eric thought he was suffering another psychotic break.

In a rare lucid moment, Max had taken Eric's backup weapon and shoved him to his knees. Five years ago, Max would have shot Eric the moment his knees hit the rooftop, achieved his goal, completed his mission, and moved on.

Instead, Max continued to mutter to himself while his gun stayed pointed in Eric's direction, but his hands were far from steady. Eric might be able to manufacture an opportunity to escape if he could distract Max.

Eric decided to start by asking him about the most traumatic thing he could. "Why aren't you dead?"

"You're why I'm not dead. You were going to stop me, but no one can." Max's voice was loud, too loud for the quiet rooftop.

"Five years ago, that girl with the fake overdose, she wasn't the first, was she? You killed others before I stopped you."

"Yes, I killed them. You didn't stop me. You set me free. Free from your stupid rules." Max's hands may have wavered, but his eyes stayed fixed on Eric.

"Why do it?"

"I gave years to the military and was rewarded with a dishonorable discharge. Shot at, marched across baking deserts, risking my life for a pittance. You and your morals were the same shit, different master. You hid behind a computer sending me to do the hard work, warning me not to kill anyone. Too much attention, too many complications you would say." He stopped pacing as he grew angry.

"Well, fuck that!" Max shouted, lashing out with the gun, slamming it across the back of Eric's head. Eric cradled his bleeding skull while Max stood over him. "Dead is less risky, and killing paid me what I deserved: cash, lots of cash, and you never knew. We were already breaking laws. Why not step it up and get the real money?"

"We were already making more than we could spend. Why did you need more?" Eric dared to ask.

He laughed. "Always more."

The mood swings from angry to laughing were quick and extreme; he was coming apart.

"You disappeared for five years, but now you want revenge." Eric remained on his knees but turned so he was facing Max. He could feel blood soaking his collar.

"I was dead. You bastard, you sent me to hell, and the demons came back with me. They're with me all the time, telling me to hunt for them. I am never alone. Your blood and Sal's money will set me free."

"Sal Marino's money?" Eric wanted to draw this out, give the FBI time to arrive.

Max dug for his phone with his left hand and held it out to Eric. He was looking more coherent than he had just moments before. The phone showed a bank account balance, well over ten million dollars.

"Sal gave me a parting gift before I put two in his skull. Millions in laundered money wired to my account in the Seychelles. The funds just arrived. Now you die and take my tormentors with you back to hell. Then I start a new life in the non-extradition country of my choice."

Max widened his stance and brought both hands up around the butt of his gun, classic firing position like at the shooting range.

"Turn the fuck around, Eric, so we can finish this." He growled, sounding precisely like the hardened soldier Eric remembered.

A loud rattle on the other side of the roof had them both turning. Eric knew this was his opportunity. He lunged at Max's knees, missing the tackle by inches.

"FBI! Drop your weapon!" One of Leia's FBI security detail vaulted onto the roof from the fire escape, his gun pointed at Max. Eric stayed down, out of the line of fire.

Max aimed at the interloper.

A shot rang out. Max's body twisted from the force of the bullet tearing into his shoulder. The gun dropped from his hand. He staggered forward.

The FBI agent was ready to take a second shot. "On your knees!"

Max lurched forward along the roof, ignoring the agent's command. Eric knew, he just knew that Max was going for the edge of the roof.

Eric scrambled after him, catching ahold of Max's shirt just as he stepped off the roof. Max roared in frustration when he crashed against the side of the building, his suicide attempt foiled.

Eric's arms strained as he held onto all of Max's weight. He braced against the low wall, barely able to hold the larger man up. Max twisted, reaching out with one hand to grab Eric's wrist. The agent knelt next to Eric and leaned over the low wall, reaching for Max.

"Give me your hand. Come on, give me your hand," the agent said. He was bent at the waist, reaching over the side, groaning as he tried to grab ahold of Max.

"That's right. Give me your hand," the agent implored, grabbing at Max's right arm despite the cast. Max refused to grab hold. "Man, you gotta reach. I'm trying to help you."

Eric's arm trembled, his grip ready to fail. Max needed to grab onto the agent.

The agent caught a handful of Max's clothing and started to haul him up. Max let go of Eric's wrist and curled his hand around the decorative scroll at the top of the parapet wall. His other arm hooked over the top.

Eric sagged with relief when Max started to pull himself over the wall.

Max stopped climbing and glared at Eric. He was more lucid than he'd been all night. "I just want to be alone."

Holding Eric's gaze, Max let go of the wall, kicking off with his feet and launching his body away from the building.

"Son of a bitch." The agent stepped forward and looked over the edge, shaking his head.

Eric stared at the spot where Max had been, stunned that he'd chosen death. He'd been a fighter, a soldier. Eric couldn't imagine him giving in to the monsters in his head. Maybe this was for the best.

TWENTY-SIX

"YOU COULD HAVE JUST ASKED me to meet for brunch or something. This is a bit much." Simms indicated the chaotic crime scene around Leia's building.

The brick façade glowed red and blue from the lights on the ambulances and police cars. Several curious neighbors huddled together, gripping coffee cups, gossiping over caffeine even though dawn was still hours away. The coroner's van partially blocked the roadway where the medical examiner's team was working to recover Max's broken body.

Eric tried to nod in response to Simms's greeting, but the paramedic stitching his head wound tugged on a suture, reminding him to keep still. Leia sat between Eric's legs on the ambulance bumper, her freshly bandaged wrists resting in her lap.

"Simms, good of you to make it this time. We missed you in Brunswick," Eric replied. "This is nothing like the side of I-95 in the middle of a Georgia night."

"Late night crime scenes are always better in the city. You can get coffee 24/7," Simms snarked, holding up his blue and white paper coffee cup as he came to stand in front of Leia.

"Fair enough. You have anything important to tell us?"

"Earlier today, Sal Marino was found dead at his home in Greenwich, two bullets, execution-style back of the head. Looks like Max's handiwork." Simms delivered the news to them like it was a revelation.

"Yep, we know. Max informed us before he jumped," Eric answered.

"Sal got what he deserved, I guess." Leia glanced away from Simms, toward where a coroner's assistant zipped Max's body into a black bag. "I kind of wanted a trial. Sal and Max should have been in front of a jury."

Simms held Leia's hand. "This is justice. Maybe not with a black robe and a gavel, but they paid for their crimes."

Leia shrugged. Eric leaned forward to kiss the top of her head, much to the annoyance of the paramedic still working on his head wound. This outcome was for the best. Max was insane. He would never have stood trial, and Eric was still processing his ex-partners insanity. And Sal…His lawyers would have cut a deal for his testimony against his money-laundering clients so fast it would've broken Leia's justice-seeking heart.

"If Max's cell phone survived the fall, check his banking app. He managed to extort a great deal of money from Sal before killing him." Eric winced as the paramedic added a final stitch to the back of his head.

"I'll get someone on it." Simms pulled out his phone and shot off a text, probably waking up some hapless FBI tech guy. "Leia, with everything that happened tonight, if you want a few more days to recover, the FBI would understand. But we'll still need your help untangling all those files."

"No. Monday is fine. I want this case to move forward. I need that." She wove her fingers through Eric's, clutching tight.

Eric had a few ideas about what else Leia needed, and he wasn't letting the Feds take point on her protection ever again. His job was not done. "Simms, don't take this the wrong way, but Leia is coming home with me. I don't trust the FBI or the US Marshals to keep her safe." He was ready to fight the agent on this point.

"I didn't expect anything less from a man in love." Simms reached his hand out to shake Eric's. "I'll send two agents to meet you at your building. Take good care of our girl. See you both Monday, New York field office at 9 am."

Simms turned away from them and headed for Reyes and Wallace, also sitting in the back of an ambulance. The big blonde guy was ready to be transported to the hospital for observation. Max had done a number on his skull.

Eric and Leia got off the back of the ambulance. He turned her around so they faced each other. He couldn't wait. The right place and the perfect time was here, now. He put a finger under her chin, tipping her head back so she looked at him. "Simms was right."

Leia tilted her head, confused.

"I love you." He tilted his head and fit his lips to hers. He slid one hand down her back, feeling the soft curve of her hip. He took his time moving his lips over hers, tasting her like it was the first time. She melted into him, and a sigh escaped her parted lips like she was content.

He pulled back, able to take a deep breath for the first time since he'd gotten out of the SUV in front of his apartment. She didn't return his declaration, but he was confident, she was his future. She looked up at him, her eyes wide, processing his words. It was just like her to need time to analyze what he'd said.

"Let's go home." Eric pulled her close, maneuvering her through the small crowd and along the sidewalk toward his car. He couldn't wait to get her to his apartment, where she belonged. He fished out his cell phone, texting his private security company as they walked to his car.

LEIA SUNK into the leather couch in Eric's apartment, wrapped in his bathrobe. She cradled a cup of tea in her hand, looking out on the pre-dawn sky. His spacious apartment was high up in a newer building, and the view over the East River was panoramic.

For most of her life, Leia lived in a world where right and wrong were easy to define, black or white, good or bad. In the last two weeks, she'd entered a whole new world colored in shades of gray. Life wasn't as simple as she'd grown up thinking. But she realized that it was okay. Messy, but perfectly okay.

She lifted a lock of her hair; it smelled like Eric's shampoo from their shower.

"Penny for your thoughts?" Eric asked when he joined her on the couch, cuddling her against him. They hadn't been to sleep yet, both too wired to try.

"I was thinking about what Simms said, that justice isn't always what happens in a courtroom."

"Leia, I think justice is rare in a courtroom. If the system were perfect… Wow, if the system were perfect, a lot would be different. Your mom would never have died in a preventable accident, or at least your dad would've gotten his day in court. I'd never have had a job. I can fix things for people because I manipulate the system."

Eric's ability to manipulate the system was lucrative,

judging by the opulence around her. The main living room of his apartment had tall ceilings and gleaming marble floors scattered with plush rugs. The kitchen where she had made her tea was so beautiful she'd been scared to leave a water spot on the flawless countertop.

"I just didn't see before how much gray there was in the world," she confessed.

"I love that about you. I've lived in the gray for so long I forgot about the colors. You are the colors, every one of them. I want color back in my life."

"Eric?"

"What I do, it isn't who I am, but it was taking over my life. I needed a reason to walk away, and you're it."

Leia turned so she could look into his eyes. "You're quitting?"

She would never have asked, nor would she have expected it, but she would support him giving up his job. She would also rest easier knowing the FBI wasn't going to be adding to his file.

"I don't have a boss or anything. If I stop answering phone calls, I'm unemployed. I have more money than I could spend as it is. Why should I tempt fate?" His expression was deadly serious. "When you told me about seeing my FBI file, my first thought was if they caught me, you would be alone. I knew right then I was done."

"You're quitting for me?"

"No, I'm quitting for myself. You're my reward." He stroked a finger down the side of her face, lingering over her cheek before he cradled her jaw and gave her a sweet kiss.

"I don't know if I'm much of a reward. I'll need protection until the trials are over. I'm mostly a burden."

"Security isn't a problem or a burden. It's just a new reality."

Together they watched as the gray dawn gave up its hold, and the sun broke over the horizon. Pale lavender and pink clouds littered the sky, a beautiful beginning to a spring day in New York.

As the morning glow filled the living room, Leia sat up and looked at Eric. And for the first time in her life, she knew with certainty that she was in love. She could never have dreamt of falling in love with a man like him, with his hard edges and dark parts. Yet here she was.

"Yesterday on the plane, when you told me your job was done, I felt like I was drifting. Like my center was gone. I thought my future was WITSEC, and I would never see you again." She looked down at the new bandages on her wrists. Eric used his index finger to tip her head up; his gaze was solemn.

He searched her face with his eyes before replying, "I shouldn't have left you to the Feds. You are too precious to me. You were left vulnerable because I stumbled. I am—"

Before he could say he was sorry, Leia placed her finger over his lips, stopping his words. "I want you, all of you— the good, the bad, the past and the future. I want the messy parts and the complicated parts. I want to figure out how our lives fit together. Because I love you."

EPILOGUE
SEPTEMBER

LEIA WAS ALMOST RUNNING LATE. Shit. She'd rushed home to get ready but would be cutting it close.

She shouldn't have stopped by Agent Reyes's desk on her way out of the office. He was a great guy, but once he sucked you into a conversation, extracting yourself was near impossible. It was interesting to learn that the Russians Oblonsky had worked for were chasing the money Max stole from Sal and didn't care about Leia. Eric would be glad to hear it.

Her FBI co-workers were a fantastic mix of ass-kicking field agents like Reyes and forensic accounting nerds like herself. She loved her new job. It also was an incredibly secure workplace, a huge plus for her.

She checked her look in the mirror near the apartment door before heading out. Her plum-colored wrap dress and killer black heels were new. Eric's flair for fashion was rubbing off on her. Her hair tumbled over her shoulders in soft curls. Her lips curved into a sexy smile as she thought about later when Eric would untie her dress and find the lacy lingerie she had underneath.

She'd officially moved into Eric's place precisely two months ago. They were meeting for a celebratory dinner tonight. For some reason she wasn't clear on, he'd asked her to meet him at the restaurant. And if the traffic gods of Manhattan were on her side, she would be on time. Maybe. She would have to ask her driver to floor it.

HE'D FOUND the engagement ring at a family-owned jewelry store near their apartment. The ring was a pear-shaped yellow diamond set with dozens of smaller white diamonds around it. The bright yellow stone was perfect for the woman who had pulled him out of his drab existence, filling his world with color.

Currently, the ring was burning a hole in his jacket pocket. He wanted to pull it out one last time to examine it and be sure it was perfect. Waiting for Leia to arrive was slowly killing him, but it was his fault for getting to the restaurant early.

The waitress stopped beside him with an ice bucket and popped the cork on a bottle of rose champagne. She tidied the table, fluffing the massive bouquet of white roses and belles of Ireland and making room for the platter of oysters on the half shell Eric had ordered.

Eric's leg vibrated under the long white tablecloth. Leia was his in every way he could want but one, and tonight he would take the first step to making her his wife. He could see their future; it was a continuous chain of shared moments.

His skin tingled, and he looked up. Leia had paused in the doorway to the restaurant. He nodded to the piano player who switched to playing *Georgia on My Mind*. He held his breath, watching Leia's beautiful face transform when she recognized the song. Their song. He rose and met her in the center of the gleaming parquet dance floor, sweeping her into his arms.

They had begun to draw attention from a few other diners, but he didn't care. He nuzzled her neck, breathing in the sweet smell of her skin. Her glorious hair trailed across his face as they swayed to the music.

His lips pressed to her ear, he whispered, "Marry me?"

She pulled away so their eyes could meet, a magnificent smile on her face.

"Yes," she whispered back.

Eric fumbled for the ring. He'd planned the proposal differently, but once she was in his arms, it burst out. He dropped to his knee, the ring box open in his hand.

Leia plucked the ring from the box with trembling fingers and held it out so he could slip it on her finger. Happy tears slid down her cheeks. He placed the ring on her finger. It was a perfect fit. Just like she was for him. He rose and enfolded her in his arms.

A polite smattering of applause erupted from the rest of the restaurant. Leia blushed and ducked her head into Eric's chest. He smiled. This was the start of the rest of their life.

NEWSLETTER LOVE

Need another dose of Eric & Leia?
How about a dream honeymoon?

**Join my newsletter
michelledonn.com/signup**

Get an exclusive bonus story to read free:
Caribbean Run: Casa de Campo

ALSO BY MICHELLE DONN

Wondering about Eric & Leia's Wedding?

Want to catch up with sexy red-head Katherine?

Read Chicago by Chance

The Metropolitan Collection Book 2

Available on Amazon.com

The Metropolitan Collection Book 3 coming early 2021.

ACKNOWLEDGMENTS

Dear Readers,

Thank you for taking a chance on me. I wrote this book during the first phase of the virus lockdown in 2020. I still can't believe I did it, and I loved it. Apparently, thirty years of reading romance novels taught me something.

I must thank my wonderful husband, who talked me through every plot problem I had. He was also a rockstar provider of coffee and madeleine cookies that fuel my writing.

If you loved the book, please leave a review or visit my website.

Thanks so much,
Michelle

P.S. DC folks, don't hate me for inventing the mansion next to the Australian Embassy. Once I had the idea, I just couldn't forget it, so I put it in!

ABOUT THE AUTHOR

Michelle Donn lives in South Florida with her real-life prince charming, two dogs, two horses, a cat, and Daisy the donkey. Most evenings, you will find her floating in the pool, enjoying a cocktail, and working out the plot of her next book with her husband.

Savannah Run was her debut novel.

LET'S GET SOCIAL!

Made in the USA
Coppell, TX
30 October 2020

40481838R00144